HIDE AND
SECRET

Helen Parker

Helen Parker

instant
ap◻stle

First published in Great Britain in 2020

Instant Apostle
The Barn
1 Watford House Lane
Watford
Herts
WD17 1BJ

British Library Cataloguing-in-Publication Data

A catalogue record for this book is available from the British Library.

This book and all other Instant Apostle books are available from Instant Apostle:

Website: www.instantapostle.com

Email: info@instantapostle.com

ISBN 978-1-912726-36-3

Printed in Great Britain.

1

When Mum said we were moving back to Edinburgh, I chucked a radge. That's Scottish for getting angry and losing your temper. I stamped and slammed doors and shouted rude words.

When I finally calmed down enough to talk to her about it, I said, 'How can it be *back* to Edinburgh? Cairo is my home, it's where we live, where I go to school and where my friends are.'

Especially Camilla. But I didn't say that. I thought that if I said her name out loud I might cry and never be able to stop. Camilla is my best friend. It's always been Ruth and Camilla, the short and the tall, the fair and the dark. We've been in the same class since we started school. I suppose that's not saying much, because it's a small school for international students and we're both twelve, nearly thirteen, so of course we'd be in the same class. It takes pupils from five to sixteen.

'But it's where you were born.'

'What?' I was thinking so hard about Cami and about how I could persuade Mum to stay, that I'd lost track.

'Edinburgh. It's where you were born. So we're going *back*.'

'But I don't have any friends there.' I tried to stop my voice wobbling. I asked all the questions and made all the excuses I could think of, but Mum had an answer for everything. Eventually I stormed off into my room.

As I went, Mum said, 'You'll soon make friends. It's a big school. There'll be lots of choice.'

I didn't want choice. I wanted Camilla.

I took out my phone to WhatsApp her. I started: *Guess what Mum's just told me?* But that sounded like a *nice* surprise, so I deleted it and started again: *Disaster! The hospital where Mum works is closing. We have to move to Edinburgh.* But there was so much explaining to do, I couldn't write it all. I'd have to tell her at school the next day.

At bedtime Mum came to tuck me in. She said, 'Sorry, Ruthie,' and I burst into tears, because I knew it should've been *me* saying sorry. Then she sat next to me, and we cried together.

Finally, she said, 'It'll be OK, honey. We'll stay with Granny McKay until we find a place of our own. And you remember the youth club you went to two years ago, when we were on a summer break, visiting Granny – what was it called? Something beginning with E? Energy?'

'Exercise?'

'Energise?'

'Yeah, Energise,' I said, and I dimly remembered joining a group of teenagers for a trip to a fairground. Mum had been a guest speaker at the church, talking about working in Egypt, so Energise had invited me even though I'd only been ten. They were friendly, and there was another girl about my age – Abigail? Alison? Yes – Alison.

But Mum was continuing, 'Edinburgh's really a wonderful city with so many fascinating things to do. There are leisure centres and cinemas and dozens of parks. And climbing walls.' She knew I loved climbing. 'You can be out in the countryside in half an hour, or at the beach. There are theatres and galleries and *fish and chip shops*!' It was a joke between us. Egyptians don't like fish and chips, but we're British.

She kissed me goodnight and closed my door behind her. I lay on my back with my eyes open. Car headlights made patterns on the ceiling. I didn't want to stay with Granny McKay. I didn't know her very well, even though she was my granny, because we'd always lived so far away from her. Anyway, her house had smelt of cigarettes. But I couldn't say that to Mum. Granny was *her* mum, after all.

I thought about Miss Samuel, my year tutor at school. She said Jesus understood if we got angry. We could tell Him about it. So I prayed. 'It's not fair. Why do we have to leave?'

2

The next day at school, I wondered how I could tell
Camilla. I'd have to wait for break, but when it came, Mr
Kuhlmann asked Cami and me to help to mount artwork
on the wall. I should've been glad, because Mr
Kuhlmann is cool, like his name. He's tall and lean with
blond hair and one earring and wonderfully colourful
clothes. Like a real artist, Mum says.

'This wall,' he said, pointing to one side of the art
studio, 'is for your year. As the season changes, we'll add
more, showing a progression, so that by Easter it will be
a glorious…' He stretched out his arm to demonstrate,
and it was then that I burst into tears.

'Ruth! Whatever's the matter?' His arm dropped to his
side, and he stared at me. I couldn't answer. He looked at
Cami. 'Camilla? What happened?'

'I don't know!' Cami said, and put an arm round my
shoulder. 'Ruthie! What's wrong? Is it your mum? Is she
OK?'

I nodded, then shook my head, and sniffed and
hiccupped. Mr Kuhlmann said, 'Now, sit down and let's
see if we can help.' So I had to sit down and explain that I
wouldn't be there by Easter, that we'd be gone – to
Edinburgh!

Mr Kuhlmann said some nice things about how much I'd be missed, and that I'd soon settle in to my new school and all that kind of stuff. Then he sent me and Cami out to sit in the sun and eat our break snack.

We went out, but of course I couldn't eat anything. Once we were outside, all Cami's questions came spilling out. 'When are you going? *Why* are you going? Doesn't your mum like it here any more? What about your education? This is a very good school. Why can't you continue here? Doesn't your mum realise that it would be awful to take you away just now? Couldn't she home-school you? Jack and Annabelle are home-schooled, you know, and…'

'But they've got a dad. Their dad goes out to work while their mum stays at home.'

'Oh, Ruthie! I'm so sorry. I shouldn't have…'

'It's OK,' I said.

I was so small when Dad died, I don't remember him. I sometimes miss having a dad, but it's not the same as missing a person.

'Well, couldn't your mum find a job in a different hospital?'

'She's tried. Most of the hospitals are Muslim. Not every clinic wants foreign nurses, especially Christian ones.'

'But there must *something* she could do.'

Then I got defensive, because even Cami isn't allowed to criticise my mum. I knew I'd said exactly the same things to Mum as Cami was saying to me but, well, we're a team, Mum and me. Team Lawrence. We've had to be. But then, so are Cami and me. I began to cry again.

Our school was a Christian school, and in assembly at the beginning of each school day, our head teacher used to say a prayer for any family that was facing changes. Sometimes the changes were good, like a new baby or someone getting a new job. Sometimes they were bad, when anybody was sick, or they were going to leave and move away. In my last week, the head teacher prayed for me and Mum. Everyone closed their eyes and I felt Cami grip my hand tightly. I tried to believe that God really did have good things in store for me.

The year before, we'd had a school trip to the Red Sea. It was brilliant. We swam and snorkelled and there were little fish that were so brightly coloured I'd thought they were plastic! They were like Disney cartoon fish, but they were real. We collected shells and I found a smooth heart-shaped stone. Back at school, Miss Samuel suggested I write a Bible verse on it. 'Here's one to keep in mind for your whole life,' she said. '"My God is my protection, and with him I am safe."' I came across it again when we began packing up ready to move. But I didn't feel safe at all.

Cami came for a sleepover shortly before we left. It was late February, so the weather in Cairo was beginning to warm up. Mum took us out for a burger for a treat. She said we could do that often in Edinburgh, but I think she was really trying to cheer me up. We had cheeseburgers and fries and apple pie. The meal came with a small soft toy, even though we were almost teenagers. My toy was a little fluffy lion. I've still got it. I'll keep it forever.

Back at our flat, we went to bed early, not to sleep, of course, but to watch silly videos on my tablet. We laughed and laughed, even though some of the videos weren't all that funny. I think we were trying to keep the sadness away. When we went to sleep, it would be the end of our last day together. Mum didn't come in to shush us, and it was pretty late when we finally switched off the tablet and the light.

But as soon as we were quiet, we could hear that a wind had got up. Wind was unusual in Cairo. True, there was always a breeze along the Nile, and it was refreshing in the hot summers. But here we were a mile from the river, and this was much more than a breeze. It was blowing the curtains in, even though the windows were shut. I could hear bins and plant pots toppling over, and smell the choking desert dust.

I got out of bed and went to the window. Cami joined me. 'Wow, the weather's as upset as we are!' she said.

I laughed. 'Usually, the weather's bright and sunny and hot, even if I feel gloomy or cross or scared! But you're right. It's different tonight.'

The wind was trying to rearrange everything. There were occasional flashes of lightning. In their brief brilliance, we could see clouds that looked orange. But there was no rain.

Now there were pieces of trees joining the race of debris dashing down the road. With a brief knock, Mum came into my bedroom and joined us at the window. She put an arm around each of us. 'How awful to be homeless in this,' she said. 'Imagine living in one of those refugee camps, with only a canvas awning around you.'

I shuddered. I'd never thought much about refugees, though we heard plenty about them on the Egyptian news channel every day.

Mum often seemed weighed down by other people's troubles. Maybe all nurses were like that, or maybe it was just Mum. Occasionally she spoke about her patients. She never named them, of course, but at times I felt she carried their problems, never mind any of her own. Sometimes we could hardly manage ourselves. What could *we* do to help refugees?

Eventually, the wind dropped as suddenly as it had started. 'There'll have to be such a clean-up in the morning,' Mum said. 'But it's time for sleep now, girls.'

She kissed the tops of our heads and went back to her room. Cami and I didn't talk any more. We got back into bed, but I didn't sleep for ages. I don't think Cami did, either. I could hear her shuffling around in her bed.

In the morning, Cami's parents came with her little brother, Alexander, to collect her. We had made a vow to each other that we wouldn't cry, but that we would keep in touch with each other via WhatsApp every day.

When she'd gone, Mum and I began to clear up. There was a thick layer of sandy dust on everything. A cloth duster wasn't enough. We had to sweep all the furniture first with a brush and dustpan. I began with my own room, while Mum began with the kitchen. When I got to the windowsill, I found Cami had written a message in the dust with her finger. *I will miss you. Sisters always.* I took a photo of it before I cleaned it off.

3

When we first arrived in Edinburgh, we moved in with
Granny McKay. It wasn't as bad as I'd feared. She tried
not to smoke in front of us, but went out into the garden.
She made bacon sandwiches often for Mum. You can't
buy bacon in Cairo, and Mum always said how she
missed it. Granny gave me the choice of television
channel, even though I didn't know what to choose,
because all the programmes were different from the ones
I was used to. But she was obviously trying to make us
happy to be back.

Mum spent a long time on the internet looking for a
place for us to live. I was in the kitchen helping Granny
prepare a salad when Mum called, 'Ruthie! I think I've
found it. Come in here and have a look.'

I left the tomatoes on the chopping board and went to
peer at the site she was looking at. It was a house, not a
flat – a sweet little house with tubs of flowers outside.
The site gave us a virtual tour. There were two
bedrooms, a cosy living room painted lemon yellow, a
kitchen with new shiny units, and big enough for a table
and chairs. It even had a tiny back garden. I liked it.

'What d'you think, Ruthie? Shall I phone and ask if we
can go and see it?'

I agreed, and the very next day we went round.

Mum followed the GPS and parked outside. We got out of the car and went up to the house and rang the doorbell. A woman in a smart navy suit and heeled shoes opened the door and introduced herself as the property agent. After showing us each room briefly, she let us wander around on our own. It already had a few bits of furniture, and Granny had some of our stuff stored in her garage. I found the bedroom that would be mine. It looked out on the little back garden, and in the distance I could see the Pentland Hills. It was very different from Cairo – much greener. We drove straight to the property office, and I played a game on my phone while Mum signed the papers.

Granny was both happy and sad. 'You'll enjoy having your own place, but I'll miss you.'

'Come and visit often, Granny,' I told her. 'It's not very far.'

I messaged Cami: *Granny Mac is OK really but got own house now. Come visit!*

4

School was a different matter. I went into Year 8 but I found it's called S1, Secondary One, in Scotland, because in Year 7 you're still in primary school. Mum said it was a good time to move, because in S1 no one would have made their firm friendships yet, and I'd be able to fit in easily. She was wrong. The others had all had six months together already, but worse than that, they had known each other *forever* in their primary schools.

Our class tutor sat me next to a girl called Lucy, who was given the job of looking after me for the first few days. It was just as well, because the building was enormous, and every lesson was in a different room. I'd have got lost a dozen times a day without her. She told me the names of the teachers – a different one for each subject. I'd got them all muddled up by the end of the first day.

Lucy wore turquoise nail polish, even though we weren't supposed to with school uniform. Every teacher told her to take it off as soon as she got home, and she said, 'Yes, miss,' but the next day she was still wearing it. Her skirt was so short you could see the top of her tights. It was a surprise to me. Girls in Cairo never dressed like that.

'Don't we get a desk or a drawer or something? Or a coat peg?' I asked her.

'What for?'

'To leave our books in and hang our jackets up.'

'Nah. Ye shouldnae leave anything lying aboot. Someone'll nick it.' She looked at me as if I was stupid.

'So we have to wear our coats and carry all our books all the time?'

'Aye, if ye dinnae want to lose 'em. Ye'll get used to it.'

So I got used to it. In fact, it was so cold, I wore my jacket most of the time anyway. I learned to sort out, the night before, which books I'd need, and take only those. I got it wrong from time to time, but I didn't get a row. I think the teachers were going easy on me because I was new.

I found that some S1 classes learned German and others learned French. I was in S1 Napier. My class was in the French group, which was a relief, because we'd learned a bit of French in Cairo, but no German.

Lucy led me to the classroom for French. The name on the door was 'Madame Robertson'. Not French, then. But as we filed in and sat down, I noticed there were two teachers and one was very young and pretty. 'Who's that?' I whispered to Lucy.

'Mademoiselle Amélie. She's French. She's an *assistante*. French for gap year student.' The boys were clowning around as they passed her, hissing or primping their hair or saying, *'Bonjour Mamselle,'* in a dreamy voice.

Madame Robertson spotted straight away that I was new and welcomed me in French. *'Bonjour, ma petite. Comment tu t'appelles?'* (Hello, dear. What's your name?)

I was taken off-guard, but I managed to reply, *'Je m'appelle Ruth.'* (I'm called Ruth.)

Madame Robertson's eyes lit up. *'Et tu viens de…?'* (And you come from…?)

'Je viens d'Egypte,' I replied. (I come from Egypt.)

'Ah! Enchantée. Je te souhaite la bienvenue.' (Ah! I'm delighted. Welcome.)

'Merci,' (Thank you) I said, and felt myself blushing. I sat down and stared hard at the desk, but Madame Robertson was clearly on a roll.

'Et l'arabe? Tu parles arabe?' (And Arabic? Do you speak Arabic?)

'Un peu.' (A little.) By now I could feel the whole class staring at me. I was hoping desperately that she wasn't going to ask me to say anything in Arabic.

At that moment a boy on the other side of the classroom knocked his chair over and Madame Robertson's attention was taken up by the minor commotion. Lucy showed me where the class had got to in the text book, and the lesson began properly.

In the last five minutes we played a game. Madame Robertson had written the words for some jobs on the whiteboard – *fermier, secrétaire, médecin, insituteur…* (farmer, secretary, doctor, teacher…) Then she gave us a clue. *Il travaille avec les vaches.* (He works with cows.) We had to guess the job. I found the game easy, but I kept my head down and my mouth closed.

Slowly, quietly, one of the boys at the back began to whisper, 'Ruth, Ruth, Ruth,' and others joined in, until half the class was chanting my name. I began to sweat and my heart was thudding with embarrassment.

Then a wonderful thing happened. Mademoiselle Amélie stood up and named the boy who had started the chant. She was tall, and although she was smiling a steely sort of smile, there was no doubt about who was in charge. She motioned for the boy to stand up, while she repeated the question. In French. And waited until he answered. In French. Lucy smirked at me. I grinned back and felt better.

At the end of the lesson, as we filed out of the classroom, I glanced towards Mademoiselle Amélie. She nodded and smiled briefly. I smiled back my gratitude and walked quickly on.

At break on the first day, Lucy shoved her stuff into her bag at top speed as soon as the bell went. 'Come on!' she told me.

'Where are we going?' I tried to keep up as she weaved her way along the corridor and outside, across a courtyard, pushing past hundreds of school students to join three other girls who were sitting on a low wall outside another exit, a door labelled West Annexe.

'This is Ruth,' she told the others. 'She's new.'

The others said 'Hi' without taking their eyes off the door. Another bell sounded, the door opened and a crowd of students spilled out, opening packets of crisps and cans of juice as they went. They were older than us – S3 or S4. The boys were laughing and jostling each other, but stopped when they spotted us and began to nudge each other. Lucy and the others said 'Hi' – they knew all the boys' names – and the boys said 'Hi' back, using chat-up lines that made Lucy and the others giggle.

When they'd gone, one of the girls asked me, 'You got a boyfriend, then – er – Ruth?'

I opened my mouth to say no, but I suddenly realised that it might be safer, with this group, to give a different answer, to avoid hassle. So I said, 'Well, there was this boy in Cairo, where I used to live.'

'What's his name?'

'Alexander.'

'You still keep in touch with him?'

'Well, more with his sister, really.'

'Yeah. Then the parents don't make a fuss, eh?'

I smiled. I didn't let on that Alexander was my best friend's brother and that he was six years old.

Me to Cami: *School is weird. Huge. Confusing.*
Cami to me: *School here is weird too cos U R not here.*

I began to realise that Lucy didn't have any special friends. Maybe that was why the teacher gave *her* the job of showing me around. She wasn't an easy person to be with. She could be grumpy and moody, but I was determined to try to be a good friend to her, and chat to her at break time. It was hard going, because all she talked about was make-up, and rock bands that I didn't know.

I decided to keep a diary. It became my way of letting off steam quietly. I didn't want to discourage Mum by telling her about all the difficult things because, after all, everything was new for her as well, so I only told her a few of them. I'd learned my 'Protection' verse off by heart through reading it so often. 'My God is my protection, and with him I am safe.'

But everything was strange and new, and I didn't feel safe at all. Instead, I looked forward to the moment each evening when I'd swap messages with Cami.

Cami to me: *Got new friends?*

I thought for a long time before writing: *Lucy. She only has her mum. Like me.*

5

One afternoon – we'd been back a couple of weeks – I got home from school about quarter past four as usual. Mum hadn't been on shift. If she was home when I got back from school she was usually ironing or cooking, but that day she was glued to the computer and frowning.

'Hi, Mum. What's up?'

She leaned back, sighed and rubbed her face with her hand. 'There's this guy on the ward – Yusef – we call him Joe. He's a refugee. We think he's Palestinian. It's the strangest thing – I recognise him!'

'You *recognise* him? How?'

'Years ago, when you were a baby, he was a student. It was when we were living in Damascus and Dad was working at the hospital there. Yusef – Joe – had taken a job as a porter to pay for his studies. He would sometimes come to our house for a meal. We used to feed the students because they were always starving! But Dad liked Joe – said he was a good, hard worker and he'd do well and go far. He even used to wash the dishes for me sometimes. I asked Joe if he remembered Dr Rob, and there was a sort of flash of recognition. Now he calls me Mrs Rob.'

She paused, and I knew she was thinking about Dad. I always felt awkward at those moments, because I couldn't remember him. 'So…?'

'Sorry, love. So Joe's going to be discharged from the hospital tomorrow or the next day, but…'

'But what?'

'But he doesn't have anywhere to go, and I'm supposed to sign his discharge papers.'

'Well, where did he come from? I don't mean Damascus, I mean…' I didn't know what I meant.

'No one seems to know. We think he may have come across the Mediterranean in one of those rubber dinghies, then stowed away in a truck and travelled right across Europe. He was in a terrible state when he was first admitted to the hospital.'

'Is that what he told you?'

'Thing is, pet, he doesn't speak English.'

'Doesn't speak English? Well, what *does* he speak?'

'Some sort of Arabic. Your dad spoke it a little bit, but we always had an interpreter at the hospital in Damascus, then later in Cairo, too.'

'Isn't there anyone at the hospital here who can speak Arabic?'

'Yes, there's an Egyptian woman. But when she asked Joe what had happened to him, he wasn't able to say anything. She reckons he has some sort of memory loss. Amnesia.'

'So where will he go?'

Mum pushed the laptop back and rested her elbows on the table. She ran her fingers through her hair. 'He doesn't have any papers. No passport. Nothing. I've heard about those reception centres for asylum seekers.

They can be quite rough. The people get housed, but they don't know anyone, or how things work here.'

'What sort of things?'

'Well, like the buses. And money – how much things are worth. You know how in the Middle East you're expected to barter for things? The seller asks for a high price, you suggest a lower one, and you finally agree on a price somewhere in the middle. You don't do that here.'

She paused and closed the laptop. 'I was looking for temporary accommodation for him but everything's very expensive and I'm not sure what's the right sort of place for Joe just now. He just needs somewhere to convalesce.' She stood up. 'Anyway, let's make our dinner. I'll come up with something in the morning.'

So we had dinner, then we watched a television programme together, though I could tell Mum's mind wasn't on it. She kept looking at her phone, and once or twice she got up to stare out of the window.

Just after nine o'clock I was about to go and get ready for bed, when she suddenly exclaimed, 'Ah! I might've cracked it!'

'What?'

'Might've found somewhere Joe could stay just for a while.'

'Where?'

'Well, there's a guy… You go and get ready, love. I just need to make a phone call then I'll explain when I come to say goodnight.'

I could hear Mum on the phone while I was brushing my teeth, and when she came upstairs ten minutes later, she was pink and smiling. 'I think I'm just about to do two people a good turn! There's a group of medical students who do the rounds on the ward with one of the consultants. One of the young guys is called Oliver. He's really excited because he's off to India next week to do his elective.'

'His what?'

'Elective. It's a practical work placement that medical students go on, in a hospital. Lots of them choose to work abroad because they get a variety of experience. Different from here. We had one or two elective students in Cairo. I told him about them and we swapped phone numbers in case he had any questions.'

'So did you call him just now?'

'Yes. I reckoned his flat might be empty while he's away.'

'And you thought Joe might be able to stay there?'

'Yes! And I was right. And Oliver said he'd be very happy for Joe to stay there for a bit because it's not good to leave property empty. He knew who I meant. He met Joe on the ward. Said Joe doesn't even need to pay him rent, because he's paid for the flat until the end of the year. It belongs to his uncle who works abroad and only comes back at Christmas. Oliver's just glad to be able to help and to have someone look after the place. And what's more, it's not far away – just the other side of your school, in fact.'

Three days later, Mum met me on my way home from school. We went round to Oliver's flat and made up the bed with clean sheets for Joe. We put fresh towels in the bathroom.

We had to do a fair amount of cleaning. 'I don't think Oliver knows what a vacuum cleaner is!' Mum said. She looked around. 'Anyway, it's pretty good now.'

'But what about Oliver?' I asked. 'You said he doesn't leave for India till next week.'

'He's staying with a friend for the last three nights before he flies.'

Mum had bought a couple of shirts and a sweater for Joe from the local charity shop, and some new underwear. She'd also bought a carrier bag of groceries – milk and cereal and stuff like that. She was preparing to stock up the food cupboard for him.

The following day, Joe was discharged from hospital.

'I took him to the flat to settle in,' Mum told me when I arrived home from school. 'He wanted to rest. I told him we'd collect him later and bring him here for a meal. Had to write the time and mime eating a plate of food! Do you want to come with me, or stay here and wait?'

'Does he have to come here?' I was glad that Mum had found a place for Joe to go, but did he have to come round to *our* house?

Mum put her arm round me. 'I know it's hard, love, but he's got no one. We both know what it's like being foreigners in a strange place.'

'But you and Dad had a job! We had a home, and I went to school. And it was all *normal.*'

'I know. We had it easy. But it's not easy like that for everyone. We shouldn't turn our backs on people when we could help them.'

I knew she was right. But I also knew how soft-hearted Mum could be. She took on other people's problems when she had enough of her own. Sometimes I wished she would just – well – mind her own business! Finally, I growled, 'OK. I'll stay here and wait for you to bring him.'

'Thanks, love.' She gave my shoulder a squeeze. As she left, she added, 'And please try to be nice.'

I don't know what I'd expected, but the man who followed Mum into our house fifteen minutes later wasn't at all like the picture I'd built up in my mind. I think I'd imagined a dirty old tramp, but Joe was tall and skinny, with clean, shiny, dark brown hair and huge, frightened, dark eyes. My anger drained away a little.

'Joe, this is my daughter, Ruth,' Mum said.

'Hello, Ruth,' he said, and stretched out a hand to shake. His fingers were long and lean, like a pianist's. His 'th' sounds were not very clear, so my name sounded like Roose. I couldn't help smiling. He smiled back shyly.

Mum had made a chicken casserole. We sat at our little kitchen table and Mum tried to teach Joe some English words: knife, fork, plate. He concentrated really hard and laughed at his own mistakes. When Mum started to clear the table, he helped, and picked up a cloth to dry the dishes as she washed.

I took out my maths homework and put my books on the table. When the washing up was done, Joe sat down again and stared at my maths for what seemed like a long time. Then he took a pencil and drew a little arrow to a piece of my working, changing the numbers very faintly. I looked at it again, and sure enough, I'd made a mistake.

'Thanks, Joe,' I said reluctantly, and he smiled warmly.

I stayed at home while Mum took him back to the flat.

'Hope he's comfy enough, and warm,' Mum said later when we went upstairs to bed. I sat on Mum's bed for a long time after I should have been asleep, and we chatted. She told me that there was a place in Glasgow where asylum seekers were housed temporarily. That was the nearest place, and Mum reckoned there was no guarantee that he'd be put there anyway. Could be *anywhere.*

'He's quite – um – fragile,' she said. 'He may have a vague memory of your dad, but I don't think he remembers much else. I don't think he has any more idea than we do what he's doing here. His memory has been damaged. I'd like to see him a bit stronger before we register him and risk his being placed somewhere else.'

'He hasn't done anything wrong, has he, liked robbed a bank or hijacked a plane?' I was sort of joking, but Mum wasn't laughing.

'I'm pretty sure he hasn't. I know your dad said he was a good worker. But the government might say it's wrong for him to be in Scotland without a passport or visa. Though it's certainly not wrong to care for strangers.'

We often used to say a prayer together at bedtime, so we prayed for Joe to make a complete recovery and for Mum and me to know how to help him. But then she swore me to secrecy. 'Better if you don't tell anyone about him, love. Not till we can be sure he's strong enough to make his own way. Those places they put them in – they're not easy. He wouldn't know anyone. He wouldn't be able to talk to anyone.'

'But he doesn't…' I began, but Mum went on, 'Not everyone is happy to have asylum seekers in their neighbourhood, so they're not always friendly. So please, love, promise me?'

'Not even Cami?'

'No, not even Cami. If you tell anyone, it might get Joe into trouble.'

I must have looked worried, then, because Mum gave me a big hug and said, 'He can be our secret. Just ours!' And she smiled that special smile that she kept only for me.

I wrote a lot in my diary before I went to sleep, then I messaged Cami.

Me to Cami: *Long hard day.*
Cami to me: *Missing you.*

6

I looked forward to Friday evenings because that's when Energise met. Mum had made enquiries about the club and I joined as soon as we arrived in Edinburgh. It started at six o'clock with a drink of juice and some fruit or crisps and a game that people could join in with as soon as they arrived. We met in the big hall behind our church.

Mum drove me there and offered to come in with me the first time. I refused because I didn't want to look like a wimp, though I wished I was going in with a friend. I waved as she drove away, and hovered for a moment in the doorway, plucking up courage. Then two kids, a boy and a girl, arrived on foot.

'Hello,' said the girl. 'Are you coming to Energise?'

I recognised her. 'Um, yes. Are you…?'

'Alison,' she said, 'and this is my brother, Daniel. Have you, er…' She was squinting, probably trying to think where she'd seen me before.

'I'm Ruth. I came about two years ago. I remember you! We're back here now. To live, not just visit.'

'Yay! Great!' she said. 'Which class are you in at school?'

'S1 Napier.'

'Ah. We're in S1 Guthrie. How's it going?'

I pulled a face. 'Very different from what I'm used to. Our school in Cairo was much smaller. Much, um, friendlier.' I told her about the incident in the French lesson. 'I wasn't trying to look clever. I was just answering the questions. But the teacher went on and on. I think the other kids thought I was showing off.'

'Do you have Madame Robertson?' she asked. I nodded. 'She's quite sweet, usually. Are you good at French?'

'Not particularly. Maybe I know a bit more French than the others do because our classes were so much smaller and it's easier to learn in a small class.'

'You'll get there. Everyone'll get used to you and you won't be new any more. Come on in and I'll introduce you to Aimee and Nathan.'

Aimee and Nathan were a young married couple, probably in their twenties. They were very friendly and introduced me to some other kids, but without making a big deal of it.

'What happens? I mean, what do you do at Energise?' I asked Alison.

'Oh, lots of games. And food. And Question Box time.'

'What's that?'

'It's a kind of discussion. We have one question each week. Anyone can put a question in the box, but it has to begin with, "What do you think about...?"'

'What sorts of things?'

'Oh, like, "What do you think about racism? What do you think about prayer? What do you think about refugees? What do you think about cheating?" Someone once put in a question, "What do you think about chips?" But Nathan threw that one out!'

Alison looked after me that first evening. I learned that she played the flute and loved reading but hated eggs and that her favourite colour was green. Daniel was her twin and they were both very sporty.

Charades was one of the most popular games. The clue, that first time, was that we had to mime a film. Daniel was keen to go first. He covered his ears with his hands and raised and flapped his elbows.

'Dragon? *How to Train Your Dragon*?'

Daniel shook his head. He stretched out one arm in front of his nose.

'*Dumbo*!'

'Yes!' Daniel grinned and sat down.

A girl I didn't know had the next turn. She wrapped her arms around herself and shivered.

'*Frozen*!'

'Too easy,' someone complained.

The next turn was Alison's. She cupped her hands round her mouth and pretended to shout.

'Scream?'

'Yell?'

'Holler?'

'Shriek?' Thumbs up. Alison made hand signals for *shorter*.

'Shree?' Everyone laughed.

'*Shrek*?' I suggested.

'Yeah!' Alison gave me a clap. I was relieved to be able to join in.

At six-thirty, burgers were delivered with a choice of salad, and we all helped ourselves and sat at round tables. Nathan and Aimee poured more juice for everyone and we chatted. Aimee sat at my table and asked me about myself. When the others heard I'd come from Egypt, they asked about the pyramids and the Nile and whether there were crocodiles. Daniel got up and did a good impression of a sand dance, and everyone laughed.

After we'd finished, it was Question Box time. One of the boys took a piece of paper from a shoebox decorated with question marks and smiley faces and read it out for discussion: 'What do you think about pollution?'

'It's horrible.'

'Like – rubbish in the sea is killing wildlife.'

'We use too much packaging.'

'But plastic bags keep stuff cleaner. They're OK if you put them in the bin instead of making litter.'

'But they don't biodegrade. Takes hundreds of years before they rot.'

Aimee asked everyone, 'Is there anything *we* can do to reduce pollution?'

'My dad always tells me I should walk to school so he doesn't have to use the car to give me a lift.'

'And *do* you walk to school, James?' Nathan asked.

'Well...'

'He gets up too late!' Daniel said, and James smiled shyly and admitted it.

Lots of people pitched in, and occasionally Nathan called a halt so that a quieter person had a chance to comment. I didn't join in with the discussion, but I enjoyed it. They teased each other a bit, but no one was unkind. Nathan and Aimee listened and sometimes asked questions, and some people came up with really good ideas. The group agreed to spend an hour one Saturday picking up litter in the local park. 'It won't save the planet,' Nathan said, 'but every little helps.'

After Question Box time, all the tables and chairs were stacked at the edge of the hall and we played ball games. Everyone was competitive but good-humoured. Alison and Daniel were really good. Basketball was their favourite.

At the end, Mum picked me up. 'How was it?' she asked.

'It was great! Everyone joined in, and Nathan and Aimee – they're the leaders – made sure that no one got left out. And we had burgers. And I got the answer right in one of the games.'

'Did you make any new friends?'

'Yes! I remembered Alison, and I think she remembered me. She's really tall now. And good at basketball. And her brother, Daniel, is her twin.'

'Do they look very alike?'

I thought about it. 'Well, they're both tall and skinny and…' There was something else about them, '… they laugh the same!'

We had laughed a lot during the evening. I decided that Fridays were my best days. Energise was such a good way to forget about school and begin the weekend.

7

Lucy lived in the same direction as me, so we usually walked the first part of the way home from school together. At school everyone had been talking about the Spring Disco. Apparently it was an annual event for S1, and you were supposed to go with a partner.

'I'm not sure I'll be going,' I told Lucy. 'I don't really…'

'You can't not go!' she said.

'Um, it's not really… not really my thing.'

'Ach, girl, you'd better make it *your thing*, or you're never gonna survive high school.'

I said nothing.

'The Spring Disco! We've all been looking forward to it for a year,' Lucy insisted. We began to cross the road.

'You might have, but I haven't even been here a year,' I thought. I said, 'Anyway, I wouldn't know who to go with.'

'There's a boy in S1 Guthrie. Daniel. Went to the same primary school as me. Don't know if he…' But Lucy didn't finish, because a crazy boy on a bike came skidding round the corner. He was braking hard and dragging one foot along the road, but too late. Lucy stepped back, but I hesitated, and then somehow the boy and I lay in a tangled heap with his bicycle on top of us, wheels spinning.

I pushed the bike aside and scrambled up hastily, tugging my skirt down. I looked at the boy sprawled at the kerb. 'Um, are you OK?' I picked up his glasses from the pavement. Miraculously, they weren't broken. I handed them to him.

He sat up and took his helmet off. His ginger hair sprang out, all rumpled. 'I think so. Are you?' He stood up and rubbed one knee. I nodded but fingered a grazed elbow. We looked around. Our school bags and jotters lay scattered all over the pavement Most of his books were covered in Heart of Midlothian football team stickers. There were some on his bike too.

We both bent down to shovel our books back into our bags. I read his name on his maths jotter: Chris Miller.

'Ah, sorry,' he said, embarrassed now. 'I was going too fast…'

'I should've…' I began at the same time. We both giggled stupidly.

'C'mon, Ruth, the guy's an idiot,' said Lucy, scowling and moving off.

But Chris Miller cleared his throat:

Um, I was racin'
To hasten
I shoulda been pacin' myself
An' placin' myself
Away from the kerb…

'He can rap,' I thought. 'Spontaneously!'

'How do you *do* that?' I asked.

He just grinned and cleaned his glasses on his jumper.

'If you're sure you're OK…' I said, backing away.

'Yeah, fine,' he said, not looking at me, but putting his helmet back on. He got back on his bike and rode off sedately. Before joining Lucy, I watched him take the third turning on the left.

Lucy continued to rabbit on about the disco, but a horrible creepy thought was making me shiver, like when your trainers leak on a slushy day and your feet get colder and more and more numb… 'My diary! I don't remember putting my diary back into my bag. What if he's got my diary?'

My diary didn't look like a diary. It was an old school jotter I'd brought from Egypt. Used to be my history exercise book, but it still had lots of blank pages. I opened my bag and began rummaging through my things.

'What're you looking for?' Lucy asked impatiently.

'Nothing.'

'Well, come on, then. We haven't got all day.'

But we had, and it was a lovely sunny spring day. I'd been hoping to persuade Mum to go for a walk along the canal. But first I'd have to find my diary.

Back home, Mum was in the kitchen, ironing. 'Hello, pet. Good day?'

'Not bad,' I said, and kissed her cheek. 'You?'

'OK,' she said. 'I've got Joe weeding the garden.' She nodded towards the window. 'He likes to be useful.'

I went to my room and unpacked my bag slowly. No diary. Maybe I hadn't taken it to school? But I liked to have it with me all the time. Our secret felt safer that way. I searched among all the books and jotters on my shelf. No diary. A creeping panic was fingering my throat now. That boy, Chris Miller, he must have put it in his bag by mistake. Maybe he hadn't unpacked his bag yet. Maybe it was a good thing that the diary looked like a jotter.

'Mum, I'm just going to, um, to get a book.' I sprang out of the door to dodge any questions. I jogged to the junction where I'd seen Chris turn off. I'd never been along this road. I walked briskly, glancing left and right, but trying not to stare. It brought me back to the original road a little further down. So it was a crescent. It didn't lead anywhere else. This must be Chris' road, then.

I retraced my steps, keeping close to walls and hedges, feeling suspicious but trying to look casual. An old man with a dog passed me, then a busy mum with a baby in a buggy and a grumbling toddler dragging his feet. But no one else. The houses were semi-detached, each with a garage at the side and a side gate and passageway, the sort you'd wheel your bike down to get to the back. Most of the houses looked as if their owners weren't back from work yet. But one had several windows open.

I hovered outside, hidden by the hedge. Should I knock at the door and ask if Chris Miller lived here, and if he had my book? What if it wasn't his house? I'd look really stupid. What if it *was* his house but he wasn't in? What if he didn't have the diary? That might be worse. So where was it? And if I let on how important it was, everyone would want to know why.

Music was coming through an open window. Someone must be in. I crept round the side, between the high fence and the garage. The bedroom window next to the garage roof was open, but no one could see me unless they leaned out. I was hidden. I reached the back of the garage and there, out of sight of the road, was the bike with Hearts stickers. So this was it!

As I stood there, my heart hammering, I heard a telephone. A shrill landline. A moment later a woman's voice called, 'Chris!'

'Coming!' It was that boy's voice, from the bedroom above the garage. He'd be running downstairs to the phone.

In a flash, I climbed onto the flat roof of the garage. Whatever was I doing? Was I a thief? A house-breaker? A criminal? I remembered the wristband that Mum used to wear: WWJD – what would Jesus do? He wouldn't climb onto someone else's garage roof, that was for certain, but it was too late now. From there, quick as lightning, it was easy to lever myself onto the windowsill of the bedroom. For once, I was glad to be small. I jumped down lightly into the room where the music was playing. There were twin beds, a wardrobe and a desk with some school books. I riffled through them. Nothing. Quick, quick! Now I'd got this far… I held my breath and looked wildly round the room. The bookshelves! Maybe…

Too late. The door was opening. I stopped breathing. And that agonising, terrifying moment of discovery was prolonged, because Chris didn't see me straight away, but went to the chest of drawers, opened one and took out… *my diary*!

I gasped and he straightened up so quickly he banged his head on the wardrobe door handle. We stared at each other. He flicked the music off.

Finally, he said, 'Ruth! Ruth Lawrence!' He was reading my name from the front of my jotter.

'Yes, I'm so sorry, I just came for my jotter, if I could just… sorry for being in your room, for trespassing, I just thought I should…' I held out my hand for the book, but he was grinning now, and he held it behind his back.

'Tenth of April,' he quoted. 'Met Joe. Nice hair and dark eyes.'

'You've read it! That's not fair. You shouldn't read other people's diaries!'

'It says *History* on the front.'

'I know, but that's because… Can I have it? Please?'

'Journal, is it? About your mum's new boyfriend?'

'No. It's not!' I could feel tears pricking, but there was no way I was going to cry in front of this… this…

'How did you get in here, anyway?'

'Easy. Garage roof.' I nodded towards the window.

'You're quite experienced at breaking and entering, then?'

'I didn't break anything,' I began, though I was burning with shame and embarrassment. There was a brief knock at the bedroom door and Chris' mum stepped in. She looked just like Chris, with that ginger hair.

'Oh! Hello. I didn't hear you arrive,' she said to me, then looked at Chris and lifted her eyebrows.

'Mum, this is Ruth,' he said. 'She, er, she came for a book.'

'Ah, well. Hello, dear.' She nodded to me then turned back to Chris. 'Letter for you, pet.' She handed him an envelope with a logo on it. I could just make it out: West

Edinburgh Swimmers. 'Lemonade in the fridge if you two want some,' she continued.

'Thanks, Mum,' said Chris.

'Thanks, Mrs Miller,' I said at the same time.

'Yes, well,' Chris' mother smiled. 'Name's Jenny.' And she went out, leaving the bedroom door open.

'Her name's Mrs Agard, Jenny Agard,' Chris said, smirking.

'But…' I began. 'With hair like that…' I hadn't meant to be cheeky. Chris' mum was obviously Chris' mum. But by now I was so deeply in trouble it almost didn't matter *what* I said.

But Chris laughed. 'Yeah. The red hair.' He scratched his head. 'Daddo calls her Fireball. 'Cos that's what she's like. Fiery. But she took my stepdad's name, Agard. Stuart – my brother – and me – we kept the name Miller when Mum married Daddo.'

This conversation wasn't going anywhere. I wasn't interested in Chris' family history, just in my diary. 'My diary,' I tried again.

For a diary
It's fiery
Don't worry
Just hurry
Tell me about Joe
Is he high or low?
Fast or slow?
Will he stay or go?

'How do you *do* that?' I asked, and I couldn't help grinning.

'Dunno, really. Just do.'

'Anyway, *please* can I have the diary?'

'On one condition.'

I waited.

He wasn't looking at me now. He started to chew on one fingernail. 'Well, there's the S1 disco coming up at the end of the month, and you're supposed to take a partner.' The hand that had been holding my diary behind his back had dropped to his side. Lucy's comments came back to me: 'You'd better make it *your thing*, or you're never gonna survive…' Chris must be talking about that disco. I could say yes. That would shut Lucy up. If I said yes, I might gain a bit of street cred.

'What's it about, then, this S1 disco?' I asked.

'Don't you remember last year? When we were at primary school, and our teachers told us there would be…'

'I wasn't here last year. We only moved here in March.'

'Oh. Moved here? Where from?'

'Cairo. Egypt.'

'Goodness! What were you doing there?'

'My parents worked in various hospitals… medics… This disco – yeah – I guess we could go.'

'Cool! I mean – OK. Got your phone on you?'

'Er, no.'

'Oh. I'll give you my number, and we can text and arrange a meeting time and place.' He put the diary down on his desk to get a pencil. I picked up the diary. He scribbled his number on a piece of paper and gave it to me and said no more about the diary.

'Thanks.'

'Listen, you'd better leave by the front door, otherwise my mum'll think…'

'Yeah,' I agreed, laughing with relief. We went downstairs. A small girl with tight, dark curls was hovering shyly in the kitchen doorway.

'That's my sister, Tonia.'

'Oh. Hi!'

The girl smiled.

I stepped outside and I could feel Tonia watching me. As I turned into the street, a car pulled up in front of the garage. Tonia ran out of the front door, yelling, 'Daddo's home!' The man who got out of the car picked her up and twirled her round, rubbing his dark brown cheek against her light brown one. He put her down gently and took her by the hand. They jigged into the house while he chanted:

Take your stance
To dance
We'll prance
Without a backward glance
By chance
We'll advance
Together…

The small girl danced along beside him into the house. They seemed so open and happy, I suddenly felt absurdly jealous. I tried to count my blessings, but the joy just wouldn't come. Even though I'd got the diary and Chris hadn't told on me, I still felt awful, but I was determined to brush the tears away before I arrived back home.

Me to Cami: *School disco next week. Not looking forward to it.*

8

'I don't know why I agreed,' I wailed. 'What was I thinking?'

'You'll enjoy yourself, love,' Mum assured me. 'Make new friends. It'll be good fun.'

'But I don't know Chris and I might not see anyone I know at the disco.'

'It'll be OK. It's at school, after all. Or you could cancel. Say you've changed your mind.'

'But you're always telling me that a promise is a promise.'

'That's true.'

'But I don't have anything to wear!'

Mum laughed then. 'That's what every woman says!'

'*Seriously*, Mum. What am I going to wear?'

Mum frowned. 'I've got a lovely sparkly green top that I've only worn once. I could alter that to fit you. And you've got that black skirt – though it's a bit long.'

Then I had to laugh.

'What?' Mum demanded.

'We've changed roles! I'm meant to be the one who wants to go out with a boy and wear a short skirt, and you're supposed to be the one to try to stop me!'

Chris and I had agreed to meet at the corner of his road. I arrived first, wearing Mum's sparkly green top, taken in for a better fit, and the black skirt that she had shortened for me. But I *did* have new shoes, a bit of make-up and pale pink shell nail polish.

I was five minutes early. I looked at my watch every ten seconds. It felt like ten minutes. I could leave now. No need to stick around. If only he could be late, then I'd have a solid excuse not to wait any longer. My clothes felt uncomfortable. I was sure the other girls would be wearing new stuff. I remembered my 'Protection' verse, but I felt like a jelly.

There he was! He was dressed up, too, in smart black jeans and a crisp mauve shirt.

'Hi,' I said. 'I'm just…'

'Hello,' he said at the same time. 'I was…'

We both stopped and giggled.

'Um, you look nice,' he said, not looking at me.

I relaxed a bit. 'He feels as awkward as I do,' I thought.

The school sports hall had been transformed into a spring grotto. Lamps with daffodil heads flashed yellow and gold. Fluffy chicks dangled from the ceiling. A waterfall of sparkling lights cascaded into a shimmering pool.

'C'mon,' Chris said, leading the way among a group of boys and girls jigging to the disco music. He found a space among the dancers and began to bop up and down. He looked funny. I tried not to laugh. At home, I'd worked out some dance moves that I thought were cool, so I put them into practice.

'Wow,' Chris said, standing still to watch me. 'Didn't know you were an expert!' I could feel myself blushing. 'How did you learn to dance like that?'

'School dance lessons,' I said. 'At my last school.' That was true, but I didn't want to be uncool, so I didn't let on that it was my first disco. The International School had held games evenings, not discos. 'Dance and gym have always been my favourite,' I told him. 'What about you?'

'Swimming.' Of course! The swimming club envelope.

'What's your stroke?'

'Freestyle, 500 metres.'

'Wow! You need stamina for that.'

He looked pleased. More people were arriving. 'Hi!' said a voice behind me.

I turned. It was Alison. 'Hi!' I said, immensely relieved to know someone. Daniel came to stand beside us. I began to relax. 'This is Chris,' I told Alison.

'Yeah. Same class as us,' she said. 'S1 Guthrie.'

So Chris, Alison and Daniel were in the same class. I wished I was in S1 Guthrie, too. I thought about S1 Napier and Lucy. I supposed she was doing her best to include me, but we didn't really have much in common.

The gym was becoming crowded. 'Want some juice?' Chris asked me.

I nodded.

We made our way to the dining room where juice and snacks were being served.

'So who's Joe, then?' Chris asked, after we'd sat down.

'Didn't you read all about him?'

'No. I really thought it was a history book at first. I only read the first entry, but then…'

'Honestly?'

46

'Honestly.'

I believed him. His face was kind of open. What a relief! 'He's just a friend, really. Not my mum's boyfriend. My mum doesn't have a boyfriend. Er, my dad died. He, um…'

'Oh. I'm sorry. I didn't… er…'

'It's OK. I was very small. I don't remember him.' I was used to having to explain about my dad. Chris' neck was turning red. I wanted to say something so he wouldn't feel embarrassed, but just then we were interrupted.

'Who'sh the dolly bird then, Chrish?' Chris turned. There was a group of three or four boys. One looked about our age, but the others were older. The one who had spoken was sneering and leaning on the back of Chris' chair. He and the younger one had very blond hair. Bleached blond. There was a group of girls buzzing around them.

'Nishe bit o' shkirt, eh, lads?' the older blond boy said, and he reached out and fingered my hair. I jerked my head back, and Chris stood up. The younger boy grabbed Chris' glasses, put them on and screwed his face up. He tottered around, arms stretched out in front of him.

Squinting, Chris made a lunge for them, but his way was instantly blocked by another boy.

'Give 'em back,' one of the girls said. 'He cannae see a thing wi'oot 'em.'

'Out, Somerfield! Time for a breath of fresh air, I think.' Two teachers steered the boys out, firm hands on their shoulders. Chris grabbed his glasses, polished them on his shirt and put them back on.

'But, sir! It's not fair!' one of the boys protested as they went. 'We paid for our tickets, same as everyone else!'

'Who was that?' I whispered as we watched them go. My heart was thumping.

'Munro and Mr Cox. They're the bouncers for the evening.'

'No, I mean the boys.'

'Oh, Adam Somerfield and his brother, Nick. He's in S3 or S4. Adam's in my class. He can be a pain in the neck. The teachers sometimes let brothers and sisters come, but I think that gang might've been drinking – cider or lager or something. Adam's always boasting about it. Thinks it makes him look cool.'

While the troublemakers were ushered out, a group of miniskirted girls, mascara like tarantula legs, jostled along behind. Some of them were giggling, others were objecting rudely.

'Do both those men teach at our school? Mr Munro and…'

'Er, yes, but his real name's Mr McAllister. He takes my class for PE.'

'But I thought you said…'

'It's his nickname. Munro.'

'Which one is he?'

'The tall, young one.'

'He's very tanned. Must've been on a sunny holiday.'

'He's always brown. It's because of climbing mountains. He says it's rust! He's always climbing Munros.'

'What?'

'Munros. You know?'

'Um…'

'Munro was the climber who listed all the Scottish mountains that are more than 3,000 feet high. That's nearly 1,000 metres. There are 282 of them. He wrote books about them. Didn't you learn this stuff at primary school?'

'Didn't go to school here,' I reminded him.

'Ah. Course.'

'And his name was Munro?'

'Yeah. Sir Hugh Munro. And the hills are called Munros now. Some people aim to climb all of them. My brother, Stuart, wants to.'

Climbing. I pricked up my ears. 'Wow! Sounds fun. Has he done any yet?'

'Oh, yes, quite a few. About twenty-five, I think. I've only done two,' he laughed.

'Well, that's two more than I've done, though I'd love to try! Which two?'

'I've done Ben Lomond and Ben Lawers. Stu's aiming to do Ben Nevis in the summer holidays. Munro, er, Mr McAllister, was Stu's class tutor two years ago. I think that's what got him started. Munro often goes climbing at the weekends. He tells us about it. He's usually one of the teachers who leads the Venture.'

'The what?'

'Venture. It's like an activity week you can go on at the beginning of the summer holidays. Ask your class tutor about it.'

'Yeah. I will.'

After that unruly gang had left, the dance floor seemed less crowded. The DJ included some funny games and Alison and I taught Chris and Daniel some dance steps. They clowned around a bit and made us laugh.

The evening went by quickly, and when it was time to leave, Chris said, 'I could walk you home? 'Cos it's getting dark, I mean.'

I grinned. It sounded like a movie. 'It's OK, thanks. Mum's meeting me at the end of the road.'

'Right. Um, do you... I mean... would you like to go for a walk tomorrow? Or Sunday? That is, if you haven't got anything fixed? I always have to take the dog for a walk at weekends. We could go to Cramond. Walk along the beach. Have an ice cream at the café.' He was blushing and not looking at me.

Time to tease him. 'Are you asking me out on a date, then?'

'No, of course not. I just... it's only... I always have to take the dog out.'

What had Mum said? I might make new friends. So what if I made a new friend who was a boy?

'OK,' I said. 'I like walks. And dogs. Only not on Sunday, 'cos we go to church.'

'Church, er, right. We'll make it Saturday, then – tomorrow. We could walk across the causeway to Cramond Island if the tide's out. Would two o'clock be alright? I'll come to your house.'

'No,' I said hastily, in case Joe was there. 'I'll come to yours. I know where it is now. Or we'll meet at the corner of your road, like tonight.'

'You're on,' he said.

'Here's my mum,' I said. She drew up beside us in the car and got out. 'Hi, Mum. This is Chris. He's in my year but a different class.'

50

'Hello, Chris,' Mum said, shaking hands very formally. 'Have you had a nice time?' She looked from one to the other of us.

'Yeah, it was great!' I said.

'Yes, thank you,' Chris replied. I was hoping he wouldn't say anything about the Somerfields. I didn't want Mum to worry. But she went on to ask him about his class, and what he enjoyed doing at school. Then they talked about swimming and his club, and I wanted to giggle because it felt like she was checking him out. Eventually she asked about his parents and he talked about their jobs.

When we said goodnight and got into the car, I watched Chris turn and head home. He sort of bounced on the balls of his feet. I wondered if mine did the same.

Mum was OK about me spending Saturday afternoon with Chris. She was keen for me to be able to use the buses, and she knew that going with a friend would give me a bit of confidence.

Cami: *How was the disco?*
Me: *OK. Some idiots got thrown out. But mostly fun.*

9

Chris was waiting on the corner when I arrived.

'Wow! Who's this?' I asked. On the end of the lead Chris was holding was a big, waggy, black and white dog.

'His name's Crackers. Because he is.'

'Is what?'

'Crackers. Crazy.'

'Oh!' I laughed. 'What sort is he – what breed?'

'He's a bitsa.'

'A what?'

'A bitsa. Bits o' this and bits o' that! We think his granddad was a Labrador.'

'He's great. Are you allowed to take him on the bus?'

'Yeah. He's pretty well behaved, as long as no one stands on his tail!'

After the bus ride, Chris kept Crackers on a short lead as we walked along the busy Queensferry Road. When we turned off towards Cramond Village he lengthened it, and unclipped it once we arrived at the beach.

I loved this place. Mum had brought me two or three times since we moved. The warm spring sun had enticed weekend strollers along the riverside, together with small children learning to ride bikes. The promenade was wide and traffic-free, and skateboarders and rollerbladers darted expertly in and out. There were people sitting drinking coffee at pavement tables outside the café, and the little beach shop next door was doing a roaring trade in ice creams, buckets and spades and cheap coloured balls of all sizes.

We sat on the sea wall and watched the swans that were gathering, hoping for scraps from the café, at the point where the narrow River Almond flowed into the wide, majestic Firth of Forth.

'D'you do this every Saturday, then?' I asked.

'Take the dog out? Yeah, mostly. Not always to Cramond, though. Sometimes Stu comes with me and sometimes we take Tonia. But Tonia always seems to be round at her friend Miranda's these days. Miranda lives just around the corner. Mum lets Tonia walk round there on her own. There's no roads to cross.'

'And Stuart?'

'Well, he's got a girlfriend and they've both got exams coming up.'

We sat in silence for a minute or two. Chris was gazing out beyond Cramond Island to where the river opened out into the North Sea. 'And Daddo's worried about Tonia,' he said suddenly.

'Why?'

'He was reading this article in the paper, about kids who suffer racial abuse.'

'You mean, because she's…'

'Mixed race. Daddo's from the Caribbean.'

'But there are lots of mixed-race kids in our school.'

'Yes. But Daddo – he's got this bee in his bonnet about it.'

'Has Tonia said anything?'

'No. That's just it. She doesn't say anything about school. Never talks about her friends. She used to be so bouncy – such a fun-ball. But now she looks miserable all the time.'

We stood up and walked to the head of the causeway leading to the island. I studied the list of tide times and looked at my watch. 'Seems like the tide's at its lowest just now. It'll start coming in soon. Anyway, it looks pretty muddy. Let's not go across to the island. Let's just walk along the promenade.' I didn't fancy getting stuck on that island of grassy rock as the tide came in and the sun went down.

'OK. Cool.'

We walked towards the open sea and paused to watch a grey Royal Navy ship progress upriver towards the naval base at Rosyth, along the deep channel beyond Cramond Island.

'They have to live on those boats for weeks at a time,' Chris observed.

'Who do?'

'People. Sailors. Engineers. Marines.'

'Oh. Yeah. I'd hate to. I like open spaces,' I said. I looked round at the water, the mud flats and the wide, grassy bank. 'If I have to make a long journey, I'd rather fly and get it over quickly.'

'I've only flown once,' Chris said. 'It was ages ago. All I can remember about it is the meal in neat little plastic packages, and earache as the plane descended.' He turned to look at me. 'Have you flown very often, then?'

'Oh, yes. Dozens of times. When we lived abroad, we came to the UK every year to visit my grandparents.'

'What, your whole family came?'

'Well, um, yes. That's me and Mum.'

Chris looked away sharply. 'Sorry... I forgot... your dad... Um, haven't you got any brothers or sisters?'

'No. There's just me and Mum.' I chewed my lip. 'But you've got a brother and a sister?' I added hastily.

'Yep. One of each.'

'But Daddo is your stepdad.'

Chris nodded.

'Where's your *real* dad?'

'We don't see him very often. He lives in England now. Sends us a present at Christmas. If we're lucky. Daddo is my *real* dad.' Chris kicked a stone viciously towards the sea wall. I hadn't meant to embarrass him. 'Better not talk about dads, then,' I thought.

We took the four steps from the promenade down to the beach. Crackers trotted along at the edge of the mud while we walked further up, where mud gave way to stones, sand and spiky grass.

'I love this walk,' I commented. 'We've come here twice since we came back.'

'Yeah. I keep forgetting you're new. Why did you move to Edinburgh?'

'The hospital where my mum worked in Cairo had to close, and she applied for a job at the big hospital here. So we came back. I'm getting used to it here. It's like living in the country, even though it's a capital city. How about you?'

'I've never lived anywhere else. Only Edinburgh. Boring, eh?' he grinned.

'Course not,' I said. 'Edinburgh's great.'

I meant it. I really liked the city. It was just that everything was just so *different* – the money, the weather, the food, the clothes – and the school was so enormous, and fitting in still seemed like a challenge every day.

Now the promenade became narrower and the walkers and skaters thinned out. On the beach, Crackers was being followed by a yappy terrier whose owner was calling it from the path at the top of the grassy bank beyond the promenade. The terrier ignored its owner. Chris called Crackers to him and clipped the lead to his collar.

'Let's turn round,' Chris said, so we began to walk back towards the village.

When the terrier had gone, Chris unclipped the lead and Crackers bounded off. We stood and leaned our backs against the concrete sea wall and looked out towards the many little islands dotted in the Firth of Forth.

'Have you ever been out to Inchcolm Island?' I asked Chris. 'I heard you can see seals!'

'Yeah, I have, and there was…' He stopped abruptly. Someone was throwing stones at Crackers. Chris leapt forward. 'Hey!' he yelled.

One of the stones must have hit Crackers. He yelped and began to run, tail tucked under. 'Stop that!' Chris shouted, dashing down the beach so he could see where the stones were coming from. A group of boys had been sitting along the wall fifty metres away, out of sight. They jumped down onto the beach to see who was shouting. I counted three, no, four. Then I spotted Nick and Adam Somerfield with their unmistakable bleached-blond hair. They had two of their mates with them. The biggest one had a tattoo of a dagger on his neck. Another had his hair shaved at the sides and gelled straight up in the middle, like a Mohican.

Crackers had bounded over the wall, out of harm's way. I looked around quickly. The nearest people were at least 100 metres away.

'Oh, look lads!' Nick Somerfield said. 'It's the two lovebirds from the Spring Disco. Out for a smooch. Go on, then. Don't let us stop you!'

I could feel myself blushing. I didn't look at Chris.

'Give us a break, Somerfield,' Chris was saying good-naturedly. 'Adam, can't you keep your brother in order?' He was clearly joking, trying to keep the atmosphere friendly, but Nick answered quickly, 'He's alright, our kid. I'm training him up. He's learning.'

'Training him for what?' I asked, then wished I hadn't. I wouldn't get a sensible answer from this lot.

'Wouldn't you just like to know, babe?' Nick sneered. The others sniggered, as if they shared a secret. Adam took a breath, as if to say something, but then looked up at his brother. I'd often wished I had a brother or sister, but not one like Nick. Tattoo-neck sauntered nearer and looked me up and down. He was standing too close, but I stood my ground and tried to look unconcerned.

'Well, time to go and find the dog,' Chris said casually. He whistled Crackers, then put a hand on my shoulder and began to walk on.

'Oh, don't go yet. We've only just met up,' Nick said in a syrupy voice, and the Mohican moved to stand in front of us, blocking our way. Nick stooped to pick up a couple of pebbles. He threw the first one idly into the mud of the Forth where it landed with a plop and was sucked under. The first silent, shallow wave instantly smoothed over the place. I knew that in an hour or two the mud would be completely submerged by the returning tide, and Cramond Island would be inaccessible except by boat. Nick aimed the next stone just in front of Chris' feet, and the following one just in front of mine. He bent to pick up more, but he didn't take his eyes off us. Adam's eyes were darting between his brother and Tattoo-neck, unsure who to follow.

'Look,' said Chris, angry now. 'What is it with you?'

'Not us, pal, you! You got us thrown out of the disco. Reckon you owe us a refund.'

Nick threw harder. One stone hit Chris' shoe. I looked around again. If we made a run for it, we'd never even reach the steps up to the promenade on this uneven ground.

Incredibly, miraculously, a familiar, tall, skinny figure was making his way along the promenade towards us, and he was *juggling*. He had three coloured balls, like the ones in the beach shop. He was ignoring us all completely, but walking with the concentration of a circus performer.

I couldn't believe my eyes. 'Joe!' I gasped, then clapped my hand over my mouth.

Adam followed my gaze and exclaimed, 'Hey, you guys! Check this out!' Nick dropped his stones and stared. When Joe drew level with us, he stopped walking but continued to juggle. He caught balls on his knee, in the crook of his elbow, on the back of his neck, and flicked them expertly into the air again, never breaking his rhythm. Finally, he tucked one ball into his pocket, stepped down on to the beach, and continued to juggle two balls with one hand.

'Wow, man!' Adam breathed, smiling at last. 'How do you do that?'

Joe threw a ball to Adam, who caught it. Then he beckoned to Adam to return it. Adam did so, and as he threw, Joe threw a second ball. Adam caught it easily and Joe introduced the third ball, from his pocket. The two of them passed three balls between them for several rounds, until Adam dropped one. The others laughed and jeered, but Adam joined in laughing, and so did Joe.

I glanced quickly at Chris. He was grinning. But how was all this going to end? Joe couldn't possibly understand what was going on. Could he?

Now Joe was showing Adam something more. Adam could already juggle with two balls, and Joe showed him how to add a third. Adam managed successfully for several seconds, two or three times, then he sighed and said, 'I'll have to practise that one. Thanks, pal.' He held out the balls to return them.

'No. OK,' Joe said, smiling. He refused the balls and pushed them back to Adam.

'Hey! You sure? Wow, thanks!' Adam grinned back. 'OK!'

'Here, kid, give us a shot,' said the Mohican. Adam threw a ball to him, and they kept up a rally of three balls, just as Adam had done with Joe. Nick and Tattoo-neck began to saunter off along the beach.

'My shot, Adam, over here!' Nick demanded, and Adam threw the balls to Nick. Nick and the other boys threw as they walked. They'd forgotten us. I sighed with relief.

'Thanks, Joe. You were ace!' I stepped forward and patted his arm. Then I turned to Chris. He was staring at us. I laughed, and the knot inside me untied itself. 'Chris, this is Joe, my mum's friend, well, *our* friend.' I turned to Joe. 'Joe, this is Chris.' I remembered to speak slowly and clearly.

Joe stepped forward and held out his hand. 'Hi, Chris,' he said, rolling the 'r'.

Chris shook his hand. 'Hello, Joe. Thanks for rescuing us. Could've turned nasty. You were like the cavalry in the old western films, arriving in the nick of time.'

I knew Joe wouldn't understand any of that, but I began to giggle. Chris was staring at me. 'What?' he demanded. I was laughing harder now. 'What's up with her?' Chris asked Joe. Joe shrugged his shoulders, but began to chuckle.

Chris started to laugh and I giggled until my stomach hurt. 'Nick,' I managed finally. 'The Nick of time!'

'You're crazy,' Chris spluttered.

'Crackers,' I agreed. 'Anyway, where is he?'

Chris whistled, and Crackers came bounding up to us from somewhere beyond the wall. He shook, showering us all with sand.

'Huh! Some guard dog you are,' Chris said, rubbing the dog's ears.

'Thanks, Joe. You did great!' I said again. Joe nodded and smiled. 'See you later, Joe. Bye.' I turned away.

Joe smiled. 'Bye, Roose. Bye, Chris,' he said.

By the time we reached the little shop the weather had clouded over. A keen wind had sprung up and it brought the clean, salty smell of the open sea. There was no one sitting outside now and the shop was empty. We stood in

the doorway for a moment, considering what to buy.
Chris took a deep breath:

> Look, here's candy
> sweeter than brandy.
> Take your pick
> 'cos Nick
> ain't here to trick us no more.
> Ices are sold
> though it's cold
> and old
> people prefer hot tea.
> But we
> are bold!
> We'll hold
> them by the cone while we go home.

I laughed. 'You're brilliant!'

'Nah, it's rubbish really,' Chris said, grinning.

We bought ices and ate them as we walked to the bus stop.

10

As soon as Chris and I parted, my mind kept going over and over the events of the afternoon – not just the scary bit – but what Joe had said, or *not* said. He'd spoken so little English, but he hadn't needed to. I'd had no idea he could juggle. That was brilliant! You didn't need to speak to demonstrate a skill like that. I planned to ask him to teach me, too.

My stomach had been doing somersaults. First was the encounter with the Somerfields, and wondering what they would do. I was so relieved when Joe rescued us, but then I worried that Chris would ask lots of questions. Now, once Chris had headed home, I trudged up our road more and more slowly, trying to decide what to say to Mum. Should I tell her? Would Joe try to tell her?

And anyway, how did Joe know where I was? I knew Mum was encouraging him to use buses, but – Cramond? Was he tracking me, or was it just coincidence? Did I feel annoyed? Didn't he trust me, or something? But he had rescued us from a very tricky situation. Nothing to feel annoyed about there. What's more, he left us after that, like he didn't want to crowd us. Did he understand we were trying to keep him secret?

When I arrived home, Mum was cooking. 'Hello, honey. Nice time?'

'Yes, thanks, Mum. We went to Cramond. The tide was about to come in so we didn't go across to Cramond Island.' I hesitated.

'Yes. You don't want to get stuck, do you? Here, stir this for me please, while I chop these tomatoes.' So I took the wooden spoon and began to stir the sauce she was making. I breathed in the yummy savoury smell. She carried on, 'Joe went out on his own. Took a bus. I popped round to the flat to check on him on my way back from the supermarket.'

I waited.

'He got back in one piece without getting lost!'

'Ah, very good,' I said. 'He did well.'

'That school email,' Mum said, pointing with her chin towards the laptop open on the table. 'It's about the school Venture. There's a parents' meeting about it next Wednesday. Do you want to go?'

'To the parents' meeting?'

'No, to the Venture, silly! Though I think kids are invited to the meeting along with parents. How much have you heard about it?'

'Not a lot, really. Chris mentioned it. His older brother, Stuart, enjoyed it.'

And so the Cramond walk slipped out of the conversation and I more or less stopped thinking about it.

Chris sent me a text asking if I was going to the meeting. I wanted to call him and ask all sorts of questions, but my phone had run out of credit. I used pay-as-you-go. Mum was very strict about mobiles. I had to top up from my pocket money, and I'd run out. Mum was trying to teach me money management. I thought I was getting the hang of it, but…

I hung out with Lucy at the parents' meeting. Mum introduced herself to Lucy's mum, and they sat down. Two single mums together. Lucy's mum smelt of cigarettes and her nails were bitten right down. Her hair was tied up in a ponytail, and grey roots were showing where the hair colour was growing out. I'd told Mum that Lucy was my school friend, but I hadn't said much else. I hoped Mum wasn't going to embarrass both of us. I wanted her to think I was settling well at school. She had enough to worry about already, without worrying about me.

'A Mini Venture,' the head teacher was explaining, 'is an outdoor pursuits week in the Highlands. Chance to meet students from other classes.' He stopped talking to the parents and addressed us kids instead. 'Chance to get to know your teachers outside of school.' There were giggles and a buzz of conversation. 'It's always a great week. You can try all sorts of outdoor activities, with expert tuition and, of course, you'll do your own chores. Very character-building, and you might even enjoy it!' The parents smiled and murmured their approval, while the kids groaned. But the head teacher continued, 'You'll have five days of the summer holidays up north, riding mountain bikes, pony-trekking, making rafts and learning to abseil.

'Mr Bruce from the history department will be going, along with a couple of the S1 teachers and two senior students as helpers. Let me introduce them to you.' He beckoned to the older students who had been sitting on the front row. 'This is Ed.' He put a hand on the boy's shoulder. 'Ed is aiming to go to university next year to study geology and botany – that's rocks and plants to you!' Everyone laughed, and Ed waved. He looked friendly and smiley, and he was just beginning to grow a beard.

'And this is Hazel,' the head teacher said. Hazel said 'Hi!' and when she smiled, the brace on her teeth twinkled.

At the end, the parents hung around for a while, and Mum was able to meet Chris' parents and chat to them for a while. They told her how much Stuart had enjoyed the Venture.

I didn't see Chris at school the next day, but when I was sitting at our kitchen table with Joe after school, doing my maths homework, the phone beeping made me jump. It was a text from Chris.

Outside yr door. Cn U come out?

My heart thudded. This moment had to come. You can't have a friend but not tell them anything about your life. 'Mum, Chris is outside. Can I invite him in?'

Mum paused and looked at Joe. 'I suppose so, pet, but be careful.'

'Course,' I said and went to the door. Chris was there with his bike, his helmet tucked under his arm, his face red with cycling. 'Hi. How did you find us?'

'I noticed the car.' He nodded towards Mum's old Ford, parked in front on the house.

'Oh. Come in.' I led him into the kitchen.

'Hello, Chris,' Mum said. 'You must be hot, cycling in this weather. Sit down and have some juice.' She put glasses and a carton of orange in front of us.

'Chris, this is our friend, Joe,' she said. 'He's called Yusef really, but we call him Joe.'

'Yes, we've already met. Hi, Joe.'

Mum turned sharply towards me. 'Already met…?'

Rats! Why hadn't I told Mum? 'Um, yes,' I said, 'when we were walking at Cramond. He was… he was going for a walk as well.'

There was a silence. An awkward one. 'Huh,' I thought. 'That's a good start.'

'What are you doing, Joe?' Chris asked.

'He's helping me with my maths homework,' I explained. We looked at my sheets of rough paper with figures and arrows and crossed out sums, and finally an orderly row of numbers in my neat jotter.

'Do you like maths then, Joe?' Chris asked.

'Chris, I, um, well, he doesn't speak much English, but he explained it to me like this.' I took one of the rough sheets and showed the progressive working. Joe had written out each step in figures, so I could follow it through. Chris nodded. He looked from me to Joe, then to Mum. He grinned.

'What?' I demanded.

'Nothing. Er, I think it's great, explaining maths like that. You don't need words, just numbers.'

Mum poured juice into glasses. 'Thanks, Mrs Lawrence,' Chris said.

'Call me Lynn,' she said with a warm, comfortable smile, and went on to ask about swimming competitions.

'Thanks, Mum,' I thought. 'Thanks for welcoming Chris – for being – well – normal with him. But we can't go on like this.'

Eventually, I said, 'Can Chris and I go out for a walk, Mum? It's a lovely light evening.'

'Well,' she hesitated for a moment, then, 'Yes, love, of course.' I tried to ignore the hard stare. Had Chris spotted that look? But he and Joe were studying the maths papers.

Outside, I breathed more freely. I looked along the road. An old man was walking his dog, and a few small children were riding tricycles up and down the pavement. I turned in the opposite direction. 'Let's walk round the edge of the golf course.' The sun was still warm, and several groups of golfers were out, dotted around the course, some distance away.

'Chris, I owe you an explanation,' I said finally.

'What about?'

'Well, for a start, I'm sorry I didn't tell you my address. It's because of Joe. He often comes round to our place. We're trying to keep him sort of secret.'

'Secret? Why? Who is he? Is he a bank robber? Or an alien?'

I couldn't help giggling, but then I said, 'It's not funny. In fact, it's very serious.'

'OK. Sorry.'

'He's an asylum seeker.'

'Where's he from?'

I didn't answer, because we didn't really know for sure, but I said, 'Actually, he *will* be an asylum seeker. But he hasn't applied yet. At the moment, he's, well, we're not sure, but Mum thinks he might be in Scotland illegally.' I waited for a reaction.

There was a pause, then Chris said, 'I've seen news reports on television of immigrants trying to cross the Channel or the Mediterranean in little dinghies, or…'

'We think Joe did that, and then came overland in the back of a truck.'

'But if he's, I mean, why can't he, that is, if he isn't… Sorry. I don't really understand.'

'I know. It's hard.'

I sat down on the grass beside the hedge. The lane on the other side of the hedge was deserted, and the golfers were a long way away. Chris sat down beside me.

'Thing is,' I said, 'my mum remembers him from when she and my dad were working in the Middle East. It must've been at least eleven years ago. I was just a toddler.'

'What was Joe doing? Did he work at the hospital?'

'Yes, he was a porter. Well, he was a student, but he was working at the hospital part-time to pay his way. Mum says some of the hospital workers used to come to our house sometimes. Life was very hard for them. Low pay, and hours and hours of study. Mum used to feed them up. She says she remembers Joe because he used to help with the dishes.' I chuckled. 'Still does! She said he used to sing funny songs, and keep everybody entertained. She told me that Dad used to say he'd go far. Become a leader.'

'So he's, er, a family friend?'

'Well, sort of, I guess. But he doesn't speak English, and although Dad learned a few words of Arabic and Kurdish, Mum never did. They always had an interpreter at the hospital, and they were too busy to study languages.'

'But how did he find you, if he doesn't speak English?'

'He didn't. He was brought into hospital here, when Mum was on shift. She said he'd arrived in a terrible state – starving and dehydrated, with several cracked ribs and lots of bruises. That's why she thinks he's travelled across Europe in the back of a truck.'

'Bet he was surprised to see her!'

'Well, no. Thing is, at first he didn't seem to recognise her at all. But she called him by name, Yusef, and he latched on to that. She told him my dad's name – Rob. Everyone used to call him Dr Rob. She said she thought there was some sort of spark. Maybe he was remembering or recognising something. So on the ward he called Mum Mrs Rob. Mum thinks he may have lost his memory.'

'Amnesia?'

'Yeah. Mum says there are lots of different kinds of amnesia, only she can't work out what sort he's got because of the lack of English. But she thinks it might be trauma related.'

''Cos of something awful that's happened?'

I nodded and took a deep breath. Chris didn't say anything. We watched the golfers in the distance.

'The thing I don't understand,' Chris said after a while, 'is why he's staying around here, near *you*?'

'When the hospital said he was well enough to be discharged, Mum found accommodation for him near us, for old times' sake, because she knew him. It's just temporary, until he's strong again. If she hadn't, he'd have been interviewed and sent to a reception centre while his application was being processed. Mum reckons they can be rough. More like a prison than a hotel. And he wouldn't know anyone. And she said he might be strong enough physically, but he's still quite sick emotionally.'

'Heavy!'

'I know. But I think Mum did it for Dad's sake. She said she remembered that Dad liked Yusef because he was a hard worker, and very willing.'

'Your dad?' Chris looked away.

'It's OK. My dad was killed. When we moved to Cairo. I don't even remember Damascus. I was brought up in Cairo.'

'Was it an accident?'

'Well, no. Or yes. Depends how you look at it.'

'What do you mean?'

I took a deep breath. I'd had to explain this a few times in my life. It didn't feel like anything to do with me. It just felt like I was reporting something that had happened. I looked away, to where a couple of golfers were about to tee off in the distance. 'He was… he was working at the hospital one night, when an emergency was brought in. A man with gunshot wounds.'

I looked back at Chris. He was staring at me. It's strange how we watch cartoons and TV programmes, and even the news, of people getting shot, but when you talk about it for real, it's so shocking. Mum sometimes reminds me that it should *always* be shocking. We must never think that people getting shot is normal.

I went on, 'People got shot for all sorts of reasons: for giving their opinion of the government, or the police force, for instance. Anyway, this guy was wounded but not dead, and they think his attackers tried to finish the job as he was being carried into the hospital. My dad came out to help, and got shot instead.'

Now Chris couldn't look at me. Whenever I told this story, it was like something that happened to someone else. I was just a toddler, so I hadn't known anything about it. Sometimes I forgot how it affected other people. Finally, he said, 'I'm so sorry. I don't know what to say.'

'It's OK,' I said again. 'I was very small. I don't remember him. I just look at photos sometimes. But we're very proud of my dad!' Chris looked, then, and smiled at me. 'Mum says he's keeping seats in heaven for us, for when it's our turn. We came to the UK when my dad was killed, but only for a few months. Then we went back to Cairo. But now we're home because the hospital had to close, and because Mum wanted me to go to high school over here.'

Chris rolled on to his back to watch the sky. He was quiet for a moment, then he said, 'Heaven. Do you really believe in it?'

'Yes. Absolutely.'

'But what will it be like? Angels sitting on clouds and playing harps all day long?'

'Course not, silly. No one knows what it will be like – but we just have lots of word-pictures, like a city with jewels in the pavement. No one will die any more, or even cry. There won't be any suffering there, so it'll be fantastic.'

'Where'd you learn that?'

'At kids' church, mostly, and our youth club, Energise.'

'Wow! Church. Does your mum make you go? Isn't it terribly boring?'

'No, it's not boring at all. We've got a great bunch of musicians, and the kids stay in for the first ten minutes, then we go out to kids' church and have groups the same age. And sometimes we have outings or games nights. Alison – in your class – she and Daniel go.'

Now we could hear voices approaching in the lane, the other side of the hedge. We could see two pairs of trainers. The trainers stopped. The sparkly pair stood on tiptoe. We heard whispers, shuffles and giggles. They were going to kiss! I put my finger to my lips, and we looked at each other silently, grinning. Then I started to shake with laughter. I pressed my lips tightly together, but then I hiccupped. Chris snorted and clapped his hand over his mouth.

'What was that?' the girl's voice asked.

'What?' said the boy. 'Never mind. Come here!'

'Hey! Stop that! Gerroff!' She must have pushed him hard into the hedge and run off, and for a moment I thought the boy was going to fall through the hedge on top of us. But he sprang back and ran after her calling, 'Hey, Iona! Keep your hair on. Wait!'

We burst into laughter. I giggled until my eyes watered, and Chris doubled over, unable to get his breath.

Finally, we stood up. 'Come on,' I said. 'It's getting chilly.' We ran back to the house, but before we went in, I paused. 'Promise you won't tell anyone,' I begged. 'It's so hard, trying to be secret about everything. Sometimes I daren't open my mouth, in case I let something slip. It might cause a problem for Joe, if I did. And Mum would feel guilty, like she hadn't looked after him well enough.'

'I promise.' He took his helmet from the hall and rode off on his bike with the Hearts stickers.

'You better not let me down, Chris,' I thought. But the relief of sharing the secret left me dancing into the house and singing my way up the stairs. I wanted to tell Cami how Chris wasn't sarcastic or stupid, like some of the boys – that he was friendly and thoughtful and… But that was too much to write in a WhatsApp message.

Me to Cami: *Got a new friend. Chris.*
Cami: *What's she like?*
Me: *He. Christopher. Cool. He can rap.*
Cami: *Boyfriend?*
Me: *No way! Just friend.*

11

I love those old-fashioned sweet shops where the sweets are in big, labelled jars, stacked along the shelves: lemon sherbets, sour plums, aniseed balls. On a drizzly Saturday, when I was missing Cairo's sunny, bright colours, I went to buy myself 200 grams of pear drops. On my way back, my phone rang.

'Hey, Ruth! I've had an idea. You know my mum works at the university?' I didn't, but Chris didn't wait for an answer. 'There are lots of international students, and one of those who learned English here gave Mum two books he'd finished with – elementary English. I've looked through them. They're quite up to date – good cartoon pictures, and films everyone's seen an' stuff. I wondered if they'd help Joe?'

I pushed a pear drop into one cheek with my tongue and said, 'Sounds good, thanks. Chris, you didn't…?'

'I just said your mum had a friend who was learning English.'

'Oh. That's OK, then. Listen, I'm just on my way home, near your road. Shall I come round and get them?'

'Yeah. Cool.'

I rang the bell and Chris came to open the door. His parents and Stuart were in the kitchen. It was warm and smelt of baking. Chris introduced me. 'This is Ruth, who I went to the disco with.'

Daddo stood up and bowed theatrically to me and grinned. He had the biggest, brightest smile I'd ever seen. 'Pleased to meet you, young lady!' My hand disappeared in his big warm one as he shook it. I couldn't help grinning back.

'And you've already met my mum,' Chris added, trying not to giggle about my previous entry. After all, I'd come through the door this time!

'Nice to see you again, Ruth.'

Stuart looked up from his phone, smiled and nodded.

'The books are in my room,' Chris said, heading upstairs. I followed him. On the landing, he paused. Tonia's door was open just a crack, but we could hear that she was inside, and that she was sniffing. We stood still and held our breath, listening. Was Tonia crying? Chris tiptoed across the landing towards his own door, but the floor creaked, and she called out, 'Stu? Is that you?'

'No, it's me,' said Chris, pulling a face. He pushed her door open gently and stepped inside. I stayed in the doorway. 'What's up?' he asked.

Tonia sprang up from her bed and held one hand behind her back. 'Nothing!' she said fiercely, and wiped her face on her available sleeve.

'So what are you snivelling for?' Chris asked. I thought he didn't sound very sympathetic, but I don't have a little sister. Then I remembered what Chris had said at Cramond about Tonia, how she always seemed miserable these days, and how Daddo was worried about her. Maybe Chris was thinking about it, too, because he said more gently, 'Come on, kiddo, what's wrong?' He beckoned me in and we both sat on the end of Tonia's bed. 'You remember Ruth, don't you?'

She stopped crying, and stared.

'Are you having a bad day?' I asked. It's what Mum used to say to me. It meant I could tell her as much or as little as I liked, or just nod.

'I've hurt my knee,' she said finally.

'You ought to tell Mum,' Chris said. 'She can...'

'No!'

'Why not?'

'Er, it's nearly better.'

'Let's look.' Chris stooped down and pulled up Tonia's trouser leg. I couldn't see anything wrong with her knee. Not even a scratch. 'Yeah, I'd say it's nearly better.' Chris smiled at her. She smiled back. He paused, then he asked, 'What are you hiding behind your back?'

'Nothing.'

'Show me your two hands, then!'

'No! Why should I?'

Chris sighed. 'Well, then, I'll just have to assume it's a pistol.' Her dark eyes grew wide. 'Or maybe it's a lightsaber!'

The corners of her mouth twitched.

'Or it's Frodo's ring!'

Tonia grinned.

'No! It's buried treasure that you dug up in the garden!'

Tonia was laughing now. 'No, silly, it's just a pencil case.' She showed us. It was a smart, sparkly purple case with new pencils, ruler and rubber.

'It's nice,' Chris agreed. 'Where did you get it?'

Tonia stopped laughing and looked confused. 'Um, Miranda gave it to me.'

'Oh, an early birthday present?'

'No, it isn't for my birthday. My birthday's not for ages, silly. It was hers, but she didn't want it, so she gave it to me.'

'Well, aren't you the lucky one!' Chris stood up, so I stood up, too. Tonia smiled, obviously relieved. He went into his room and I followed. He stared out of the window.

'What do you make of that?' he asked. 'She was obviously not telling the truth. Why was she so upset?'

'Do you think she could've, um, taken the pencil case from someone?'

'D'you mean, like, stolen it?'

'Well…'

I didn't like to suggest that Tonia was a thief, but…

'She knows Daddo would have bought her a nice new pencil case,' Chris said. 'She only had to ask.'

Chris ran his hand through his ginger curls and turned away from the window. He seemed to remember what we'd come for. 'The books. Yeah.' He handed them to me and I flicked through them. They looked useful, and I knew Joe didn't have any other English language textbooks to learn from.

'Are you busy this morning?' I asked him. 'I was thinking – we could take the books round to Joe now. His flat's near school. Mum's at work, so Joe will be alone and probably getting bored.'

'Cool! Free morning. Let's do it.'

12

We arrived at the flat and rang the doorbell. Joe opened the door and his anxious face broke into a smile when he saw it was us. He said, 'Hi, Chris. How are you?'

'Fine, thanks, Joe. How are you?'

'Fine, thanks!' Joe beamed, proud of himself.

'Mum's been teaching him greetings,' I told Chris.

Joe invited us in. 'Look, Joe.' I gave him the books. 'English. For you to learn.' I turned to the first page.

Joe looked eagerly and read for a moment. Then he put the book down, held out his hand to shake, and said, 'Hello. What's your name?'

'Ruth,' I replied, laughing and joining in his game. 'What's your name?'

'Yusef. Joe!' he said, grinning, and he repeated the same scene with Chris.

Chris turned to a later page with a map of Britain. 'Look, Edinburgh,' he said, pointing. 'That's us. We're here. Edinburgh.'

'Edinburgh,' Joe replied, not grinning any more. He frowned and chewed his lip. Maybe he had no idea how he'd got there. 'Edinburgh,' he repeated, sitting down. Then he turned back to the first page and patted the sofa for us to sit next to him. I pointed to the next section.

'He's a farmer.' I read the sentence under the cartoon of a man on a tractor. Joe repeated it.

'She's a dentist,' Chris continued. 'He's a builder. She's an artist.'

'She's a nurse,' I continued, pointing at the picture. 'Like Mum.'

'Yes!' Joe agreed. 'Mrs Rob. Lynn. She's a nurse!'

'Yeah!' We smiled and clapped.

'He's a school student,' I said, pointing at Chris.

'She's a school student, too,' Chris joined in, pointing at me. Then he turned to Joe. 'And you, Joe? What's your job? He's a…?'

Joe's face fell. Chris turned to me. 'He doesn't know the word.'

'Maybe he can't remember what his job was.'

Chris groaned. 'Sorry. I should've realised.'

I had an idea. 'Chris, it's only half past ten and my mum's at work all day. How about if we took Joe into town? I'll phone Mum and check.'

'Suits me,' he said. 'I'll just text Daddo.'

'Joe,' I said. 'Would you like to go into town? With us? On the bus?'

'Yes,' he replied. 'I like.'

Joe looked around with enthusiasm on the bus into town. The drizzle had given way to bright spring sunshine. 'Castle,' he pointed, as we reached the west end of Princes Street. 'Beautiful. I like.'

'Me too,' Chris smiled. He turned to me. 'He knows more than I thought.'

'It's Mum. She's been working on him, but she doesn't have much time.'

'But we've got some time to teach him,' Chris said. Suddenly I felt so grateful to him for sharing our secret – and the responsibility – that I nearly hugged him. But I didn't, because he would've been embarrassed. So would I.

Early summer tourists were already out, admiring the sights. We took Joe into Princes Street Gardens, where we bought cans of cola from a kiosk and stood for a while, watching a busker playing his bagpipes. Joe looked puzzled. 'Man,' he said, and touched the knee of his trousers.

'Er, yes,' I agreed.

Joe looked around and pointed to a woman. 'Woman!' Then he pointed to the piper. 'No woman!'

Chris laughed. 'It's a kilt!' he explained. 'Scottish men wear a kilt.' Of course – Joe thought it was a man in a skirt. I nodded and grinned.

'Kilt,' Joe repeated slowly. 'Scottish men wear kilt.'

We stood on the bridge and watched trains underneath us slowing down to enter Waverley station, then we walked up the steep path towards the castle, pausing occasionally to turn and admire the view of the city. At the entrance to the castle, we stopped.

'Have you ever been in?' I asked Chris.

'Yeah. Lots of times. We ought to take Joe.'

I looked at the ticket prices. 'But it's so expensive.'

'I know what! We should take him to the Tattoo! He'd see hundreds of bagpipers, and dancers, and all the traditional Scottish stuff. Or the Festival Parade. That doesn't cost anything. You get a kind of preview of everything that's going to happen.'

'The Edinburgh Festival? It's not till August, though.' I looked at Joe, then at Chris. He seemed to read my thoughts. Who knew what might have happened to Joe by August?

'We'd better get on with English lessons fast,' Chris muttered.

We left the castle and carried on walking, stopping to look at the new block that had replaced several old buildings that had been burned to the ground. 'That's what Adam's chosen for his school history/geography project,' Chris said. 'A fire started in a nightclub there when we were very small, and because the buildings are so tightly packed, and so tall, it spread very quickly.'

'Like the Great Fire of London,' I remembered. 'How did this one start?'

'No one seems to know whether it was deliberate or an accident. Maybe Adam will be able to tell us in the end. He was quite keen. I've never seen him look so enthusiastic about a piece of school work.'

'What's your project on?' I asked him.

'Dunno yet.' He turned to Joe. 'There was a big fire,' he explained. Joe looked blank. 'A fire,' Chris repeated, looking round. There was a billboard advertising an action film. He pointed to the picture of flames. 'A fire.'

Joe gazed at the picture and his face went very white, like Mum's when she's got a bad headache. Or maybe he was hungry. Like me.

'Come on,' I said, marching forward. We stopped beside the life-size statue of Greyfriars Bobby.

Chris patted the little bronze dog. 'Do you know the story?' he asked me. I shook my head. 'The dog's called Bobby. His owner was John Gray. He lived about 150 years ago. He used to walk the dog around Greyfriars every day. When John Gray died, Bobby refused to leave his grave. It's there, in the kirkyard.' He pointed towards the gate to the cemetery. 'Bobby sat on the grave faithfully for fourteen years, and the landlady from a local pub gave him dinner every day.'

'Fourteen years!' I patted the statue. 'His name's Bobby,' I told Joe. 'He was very faithful.'

'Bobby,' Joe repeated. 'Faceful.'

'Faithful,' I corrected, and stuck my tongue out in an effort to emphasise the 'th'.

'Faithful,' Joe repeated correctly.

We turned back towards the city centre. Joe stopped outside a butcher's shop. 'Maybe he's hungry,' I suggested. 'I know I am. Let's buy a burger when we get back to Princes Street. It must be lunchtime.'

But Joe was pointing at something. 'Haggis,' Chris told him. 'Delicious!' He licked his lips and patted his stomach.

Joe laughed and pulled a face. He turned to me. I shrugged. 'I've never tried it.'

'Never tried it?' Chris said. 'You can't be a true Scot and not eat haggis.'

'But it looks disgusting.'

'Looks aren't everything,' Chris joked. 'It's very tasty. But it reminds me that I'm starving. Come on, let's get some food.'

Returning through the gardens, we crossed Princes Street to the side where the shops were. The pavements were crowded with visitors and weekend shoppers. The warm early June sun had brought everyone out in their colourful T-shirts. The Japanese tourists were taking photos, the Americans were buying tartan souvenirs and local children were begging their parents for ice creams.

I glanced at my watch. One o'clock. No wonder we were starving.

'Come on, let's…' Chris began, but the next moment we found ourselves sprawled face down in the entrance to a department store, with Joe on top of us, squeezing the breath out of us. Scenes from television flashed through my mind: bombs, earthquakes, explosions. Terrorist attacks!

I opened my eyes and twisted my head to one side. Chris' glasses were on the floor beside him. I reached for them. Nobody else was on the floor, just us three. Shoppers going in and out had leapt back, scared, puzzled, even amused. A small, curious crowd was gathering.

'What?' I gasped. 'What's the matter? What happened? Joe? Chris? Are you OK?' I wriggled and freed myself. Chris and Joe sat up, too. I handed Chris his glasses. The shoppers began to walk on again, skirting around us warily.

A middle-aged couple had stopped. The man squatted down beside Chris. 'Are you alright, son? What happened?' The woman knelt beside me. Joe stood up shakily and looked around, dazed.

'I don't know,' Chris said, adjusting his glasses.

Suddenly I realised. 'It was the one o'clock gun at the castle! Joe didn't know, er, he must've thought…' I struggled to my feet and Chris did the same. 'It's OK. We're OK,' I said to the anxious woman. 'Thanks.' I grabbed Joe's arm and marched outside, back on to the pavement. 'Come on, Chris!' I hissed over my shoulder.

Chris turned to the man. 'Thanks, er…' Then he quickly followed me.

Eventually, Joe leaned against a bus shelter, looking like a ghost, his dark, fear-filled eyes gazing past us.

Tears were pricking the backs of my eyes. 'I think it was the one o'clock gun,' I repeated, trying to stop my voice trembling. 'I don't think Joe's ever been in town at one o'clock before. He must've thought…' A rogue tear escaped and slid down my cheek. I turned away.

Chris put a hand on my shoulder. 'It's alright. Come on, let's go.' I could tell he felt awkward. So did I. Neither of us wanted to stand there any longer, with people staring at us curiously as they walked past. Chris steered Joe and me back to the gardens, where we sat on a bench.

'I'm going to get food. Got to keep our strength up,' Chris said, and five minutes later he returned with cheese toasties and milkshakes. I picked at my toastie. I'd been ravenous a few minutes before, but I'd gone off the idea now. Joe ate like a robot. I don't think he realised he was eating. Chris left his last crust and threw it in the bin.

On the bus home, I tried to explain to Joe. 'Every day, Monday, Tuesday, Wednesday. Every day, one o'clock, you can check the time.' I pointed at my watch. 'Boom! One o'clock. Every day.' Joe just stared past me, as if I wasn't there at all.

Went into town I messaged Cami. I imagined her saying 'So what?' So I started again and wrote:

Weekend! Yay! Hope yours is good.

13

Chris and I generally spent an hour with Joe after school, except on Thursdays, because of swimming training. Chris was amazed at Joe's progress in English. 'I think he must eat a couple of pages of dictionary for supper each night,' he joked. It was Wednesday, and Joe was at our house for dinner.

'He always tries to read the headlines of the local newspaper,' I said. In fact, there was a copy lying on the kitchen table. Chris flicked over a few pages till he found an article about a local shop that had burned down.

'This was a DIY shop,' he said. 'Daddo used to love it, 'cos he said the owner gave good tips and advice. He's Polish – Mr Kowalski.' He read the name from the paper. 'Adam brought the article into school this morning and was showing everyone. Don't know why he was so interested.'

'Maybe his dad knows Mr Kowalski as well,' I suggested. 'Or maybe it's got something to do with his project. About fire.'

In the living room, Joe was watching a sports quiz show on television.

'Hi, Chris,' he said. 'They're playing tennis.' He pointed to the screen. 'He's playing golf. They're playing football. Do you like football, Chris?'

'Yes, I do. Joe, do you like football?'

I felt proud that Joe was getting all the language right.

'Yes, I do,' Joe answered with satisfaction. He turned back to the screen. There was a video clip of a rugby game. Joe began, 'They're playing... What?' He mimed the shape of the ball and shrugged his shoulders. Then he declared, 'They're playing haggis!'

He picked up a small cushion and squashed it into a haggis shape. He passed it to Chris. 'Playing haggis!'

'Playing haggis! I love it,' I squealed. 'Must tell Mum that one.'

'Rugby,' Chris corrected, laughing. 'They're playing rugby.'

'Rugby,' Joe repeated carefully.

'That's it!' Chris announced suddenly. 'Cool! Thanks, Joe.'

'That's what?' I asked.

'An idea for my project. It's going to be Scottish culture from a newcomer's point of view. All the things that must look crazy to a foreign visitor. Kilts, haggis, rugby, all that stuff.'

'Chris, you won't ever mention...'

'Not a word,' he promised. 'It's only a school project, but I might as well have fun at the same time. Playing haggis!' He passed the cushion back to Joe and they laughed again.

The next quiz question was about swimming. 'They're playing swim,' Joe tried.

'Not playing, just swimming. They're swimming,' Chris told him.

'They're swimming.'

'Joe, Chris is a very good swimmer. Do you like swimming, Joe?'

'Yes, I like.'

'Yes, I do,' I corrected automatically.

'Hey, Ruth, why don't we take Joe swimming on Saturday?' Chris suggested. 'We could go to the Royal Commonwealth Pool. It's so big, there's always space there.'

'Hmm. He hasn't got any swimming shorts.'

'I'm sure I can borrow some of Daddo's for him.'

On Saturday morning, Chris and I took Joe on the bus to the big old pool in the shadow of Holyrood Park. Having bought the tickets, we parted. I went to the female changing rooms, and Chris and Joe to the male.

I was ready and at the poolside before them. As soon as they appeared, Joe got into the water immediately and splashed along the length. I watched him, and he waved when he reached the other end. 'Wow! He's pretty good,' I said. I turned to Chris. 'What's up? You look worried.'

He said, 'Er, have you ever seen Joe without his shirt on?'

I thought about it, and felt a blush creep up from my neck. 'No. Why?'

'Is there a big mirror in his flat? Like, a full-length one?'

'A mirror? What are you talking about?'

'Just tell me. What's the mirror in the bathroom like?'

'Um, I think it's on the cabinet.'

'Is it the right height for shaving?'

'Come on! You might think you're macho, but you're not shaving yet!' I was joking, but Chris didn't smile.

'No, seriously, Ruth, is there a full-length mirror in the house?'

'I don't know! There might be one on the inside of the wardrobe door. Some wardrobes are like that. Why?'

'Well, have you seen the scar on Joe's back?'

'Scar? What scar?'

'I think it's a burn scar. If I had a scar like that, I'd be embarrassed to take my shirt off. Thing is, I'm not sure he knows he's got it. And if there isn't a long mirror…'

Joe's head popped up. 'Ruth, come. Water very good. Come.'

I jumped in beside him and Chris joined me. I disappeared underwater, emerging behind Joe. There it was, a horrific burn scar, all down one side of his back, from his left shoulder to the top of his shorts. I took a deep breath and ducked underwater again. I popped up in front of them both and said, 'Boo!' We splashed and laughed and played tig. Chris lost, because he couldn't see clearly where we were without his glasses. Finally, we raced, and of course, Chris won.

I managed to play and laugh and clown around, while thoughts of terror attacks and torture were racing through my mind. It was like living in two time frames. Or like a sci-fi movie. When we parted to get dried and dressed, I wondered what we would say to each other. Would Chris and I pretend nothing had happened – that we hadn't noticed anything? People say ignorance is bliss. Is it true? Is it better not to remember something as bad as a burn? What about telling the truth? WWJD? What would Jesus do?

But when Joe and Chris reappeared, I could tell something had happened. They were both pale, and neither was smiling. 'There's a big mirror in the changing room,' Chris murmured. 'He saw.'

On the bus on the way home we passed the site of the fire that Adam had chosen for his project, where the old nightclub used to be.

'Fire,' Joe said sombrely. 'Fire very bad.'

We didn't speak for most of the journey home. The sparkle had gone out of the morning.

When we reached our bus stop, Joe insisted on going back to the flat. I reminded him that Mum was expecting us all for lunch, but he made some sort of hand signal that I didn't understand, went inside and shut the door.

Mum was cooking sausages when I arrived home with Chris. She smiled at us, and her face was pink from the warmth of the kitchen. Chris and I stood awkwardly in the doorway.

Mum's smile faded. 'What happened, love? Where's Joe?'

'Mum,' I whispered. 'Have you seen Joe's back? He's got a terrible burn scar. Have you seen it?'

'I'm a nurse, love. What do you think?'

'How did he get it?'

'I don't know, and what's more, I'm not sure he knows he's got it.'

'He does now,' I said.

Chris said, 'I'm sorry, Lynn. Maybe we shouldn't have taken him swimming. We should've given him longer.'

'Don't worry, Chris. He knows you're a friend. He trusts you.' She turned to me. 'Now, why don't you two go down to the shop and buy some rolls so I can make these sausages into hot dogs, and I'll drive round and see if Joe's OK?'

So we went.

'I think it's brilliant, what you and your mum are doing for Joe,' Chris said quietly as we walked to the corner shop.

'But it's going all wrong!' I wailed. 'We wanted to do the right thing. It's right to look after strangers and people in need. But it's wrong to tell lies, or to be deceitful.' I felt like crying. 'Secrets should be happy things, like birthday presents and special treats.'

'Do you talk about stuff like refugees at your youth club? Er, Energise?'

'Oh, yes. And the Bible's full of stories of refugees.'

'I tried reading Mum's granddad's Bible once. It's impossible.'

'Not if you take a bit at a time. And in modern English.' We walked on while Chris seemed to be thinking. Then I added, 'Also, Mum found out Joe should have registered immediately as an asylum seeker.'

'So why doesn't she help him register now?'

'She said she was planning to, but someone told her people have to do it as soon as they arrive. He'd have to go to England for assessment, then he could be placed anywhere. That's the difference between an asylum seeker and an illegal immigrant. They might say that Joe's here illegally.'

'And if he gets found out, he'll get sent to prison?'

'Well, to a centre for refugees. Or he might be deported. Sent back to wherever he came from. He'll have no freedom, no friends, no home! And now, Mum thinks she might get into trouble for *harbouring* him, or at least for not registering him.'

'So it's doubly important to keep him secret until he can cope on his own?'

'Yes, but…'

We'd arrived at the shop. We bought the rolls, and on the way back Chris said, 'So what can you do now?'

'Dunno.' We walked on. 'We pray together for Joe every day.'

'D'you think it makes any difference?'

'I once heard that God always answers prayer. Sometimes He says yes, sometimes He says no, and sometimes He just says wait.'

We walked the rest of the way home in silence.

By the time we arrived, Mum was back and Joe was there. He was sitting at the table with his English book open.

'Alright, Joe?' Chris said.

'Hi, Chris,' Joe replied. His colour had returned and he looked a bit better. 'I'm studying.' The book was open at the past tense: I had, you had, we had; I was, you were, we were. Joe turned the page to the regular verbs: I watched, I looked, I helped. He had finished the practice exercises and had begun the page of irregular verbs: I went, I saw, I heard.

'Lunchtime, everyone,' Mum said, and Joe put the book aside.

We all sat down and ate hot dogs and salad, while Mum chatted happily and kept the mood cheerful. Joe seemed to be deep in thought. As soon as he had finished eating, he took his plate to the sink, then picked up his English book. We watched him expectantly, like little children waiting for a story.

'My name is Yusef,' he began. 'I had wife. Her name was Nadia. I had little girl. Her name was Deena.' He was emphasising the past tenses. 'I had good apartment. Three rooms.' He waved a hand round, indicating the house. 'One day, I was out. I go home, er, I went home. I saw man. He had, er…' He drew a little picture in the corner of the page.

'A hand grenade!' Chris exclaimed.

'He…' Joe mimed throwing. 'In window. Boom. Big fire. I wanted help Nadia and Deena. But no, I could not. Very bad fire. Nadia and Deena… now, they are not.' He dropped his head. A clock ticked sombrely in the otherwise silent room, and my heartbeat hammered in my ears. A single tear ran down Joe's cheek.

Mum reached out and stroked his arm gently. He took her hand and kissed the back of it.

'Thank you, Lynn,' he said. 'Thank you, Ruth. Thank you, Chris. Very kind. My friends.'

Under the table, my knee was jiggling. I felt for Chris' hand and gripped it for a moment.

So many questions were tumbling through my mind. Who was the man with the hand grenade? Why had he thrown it? What did he have against Joe and his family? What did Joe do then? But I knew this wasn't the time to ask, and I doubted whether Joe's English was up to it yet, even if he could remember.

Later, when the table was cleared and the dishes were washed, Joe said he would like to walk back to the flat. 'Don't you think we should go with him, Mum?' I suggested. 'He might be lonely on his own.'

'I think he needs a bit of space, love,' she replied quietly. 'Best leave him be.'

As the door closed behind Joe, Chris and I spilled out all our questions.

'How could he forget all that, and then remember?' I asked.

'Who do you think could have had it in for him? He doesn't seem like the kind of guy who'd make enemies,' said Chris.

'Why would they attack his whole family?'

'Do you think he can remember everything now?'

'How did he find a truck travelling to Scotland?'

'I don't think we'll know for quite a while,' Mum said. 'Not until he has more English, anyhow. Everything fell apart in Syria once the civil war started. But remember the situation in some of those Middle Eastern countries. If they don't like your politics…' She drew a hand across her throat, like a knife.

I looked out of the window at the back garden. The sun picked out the colours on the flowerbed. A light breeze stirred the leaves of our neighbour's tree. Once we were quiet, we could hear the kids next door, playing. It was a million miles from that unstable world where people got shot or blown up at random. We'd always felt pretty safe in Cairo, but that world existed. Right now. And Cami was there.

I wanted so much to tell Cami about the day, but I just wrote:

Went swimming with Chris. He's very good.

Before Chris left, I ran up to my room to find a little book
– a Gospel of Luke, from the Bible in modern English.
Nathan and Aimee had given two to everyone at
Energise: one to keep and one to give away. Chris took it
and said, 'Hmm. That looks a bit easier. I'll have to try it.'

14

As soon as term ended, there was the Venture to look forward to. In fact, I really *was* looking forward to it, even though I didn't know what it would be like. But Chris was sure we'd have a great time because Stuart had told him all about it. Alison and Daniel were both going. So was Lucy. Sometimes, at school, I wished our tutor had given someone else the job of showing me round when I was new. Lucy and I had so little in common, but I was aiming to be patient and kind to her.

Before we went, Mum let me phone Cami and talk to her.

'I'm not sure whether I'll be able to text every day,' I told her. 'Don't even know if there'll be good phone reception, but I'll take photos and send them to you later.' I told her as much as I had heard from the parents' evening and from Chris and Stuart.

'Ooh! I'm dead jealous,' she said. 'I'd love to spend a week doing outdoor activities in the Highlands.'

'Well, I'd love to be going to a Red Sea resort and swimming in the sea every day like you,' I told her, and we agreed to swap news afterwards.

It was wonderful to chat to her, and her enthusiasm took away the last bit of nervousness I'd been feeling about going.

The Venture began with a long coach journey. It was the only part I definitely hadn't been looking forward to, but in the end it was good fun. Mr Bruce told us gruesome stories from history – the sort you never learn at school. Munro organised a talent contest, consisting mainly of Ed's jokes and Hazel's funny stories. Ed was also a very good musician. Alison sang with Ed accompanying her on his guitar, and although she had a good singing voice, she giggled so much, no one could hear the words.

Eventually, Mr Bruce stood up and pointed. 'There's the hostel – the old mansion house beside the lake.'

'Wow! It's just as good as the photos in the brochure,' Chris breathed as the coach turned off the winding lakeside road and up the lane to Lochs View Hostel.

'A view of the lochs tae the front, and the hills tae the back,' Ed announced. I craned my neck to look around. The hostel was almost on the shore of the nearer loch, and a smaller one glittered in the distance. It was so beautiful, I wanted to take photos straight away.

'Curious neighbours,' Chris commented, watching a flock of sheep eyeing our approach.

The coach parked outside the front door of the house.

'Baa!' Lucy bleated at the sheep.

'They're *flocking* to welcome us!' Munro said with a twinkle in his eye.

'Now, no *bleating* about who you're sharing a room with,' Hazel told us. 'There's no *woolly* organisation here!'

'No need to *ram* the point home, Hazel,' I added, grinning.

Chris laughed. 'Hey, I can't keep up with you clever lot!'

'Ruth, I thought you were as meek as a *lamb*!' Mr Bruce put in.

'Then *ewe*'d be wrong,' Chris added with a triumphant grin.

'Mint sauce!' Lucy shouted, running at the sheep and sending them scattering in all directions, bleating pitifully.

We filed into the hostel. It was warm and smelt of furniture polish and fresh bread. Hazel read out the list of rooms. Ed showed everyone where their rooms were. I was sharing with Alison and Lucy. I was delighted to be with Alison. I never saw much of her at school, but we always hung out together at Energise and kids' church. She gave me a high five and a dimply smile.

The room was spacious, with bunk beds and a single bed. 'Shotgun top bunk!' Lucy claimed.

I didn't mind. I tried out the mattress on the single bed. The furniture was old and basic, but adequate, and the whole house had a well-scrubbed look. 'Wonder who used to live here before it became a hostel for youth groups?' I asked no one in particular.

'Lord and Lady Someone or Other,' Alison said. 'The Laird of the Lochs!'

'Great! Look. Private exit,' Lucy exclaimed, opening the window. It led to a fire escape. There was a printed notice beside the window: 'For use in emergency only.' Lucy climbed out.

'Lucy!' Alison and I chorused.

'What?' she replied defiantly, climbing to the top. We sighed, left our rucksacks on our beds and went downstairs.

The first few days passed in a rush of activities: canoeing, sailing, climbing, pony trekking. I enjoyed almost every minute of it: the activities, the freedom, old and new friends and lots of good food. And Mr Bruce was right – even doing the chores was not so bad in a group. Occasionally I thought about home, and about Mum. I wondered how Joe was getting on. I was a bit ashamed to realise I didn't really miss them. In fact, it was a relief not to have to worry about what I said, or worry about Mum worrying.

Chris was sharing a room with Daniel and a guy called Ahmed. The three of them were late for breakfast one morning, and Munro went upstairs to find them. When they came down, Ahmed had obviously been crying.

'What's up?' I whispered to Chris.

'Ahmed had a call from his dad,' he whispered back. 'Their shop burned down yesterday. All their stock was damaged or destroyed.'

'Oh, how awful! How did it happen? They often say a fire was caused by an electrical fault.'

'Dunno. But both these shops were owned by foreigners. Wonder if it was a racial thing.'

'What, you mean someone started the fire on purpose?'

'Maybe they don't like foreigners.'

'Or maybe you just think that because of what Daddo said – about Tonia.'

'Hmm. Maybe.'

Each evening ended with optional competition entries, and each day began with an announcement of the previous day's winners. Thursday's competition was a scavenger hunt. I was planning to enter.

Chris appeared as I was sitting in the common room surveying my collection of objects. 'What are you doing?' he asked.

'Trying to find a natural object beginning with each of the letters of Lochs View Hostel.'

'What have you got so far?'

'A laurel leaf, orange peel, a cone, a holly leaf, a stone, a dead fly…'

'A dead fly?' Chris interrupted.

'An *insect*,' I pointed out patiently, then continued, 'An egg shell, a weed, honeysuckle, a snail shell…'

'What about "v"? You haven't got "v" for View.'

'I know. I haven't got the second o, either.'

Chris ruffled his hair and jumped around, scratching his armpits. 'What's that?' I asked. He could be such a clown.

'A violent orangutan!'

'Well, you've got the right hair colour,' I agreed.

'How about a *very* keen ornithologist?'

'A what?'

'Ornithologist. Studies birds.' He looked around at imaginary birds, holding thumbs and fingers to his eyes for binoculars. 'Or oxygen?' He sucked in air.

'Give up! Look, be serious. I want to win this.'

He stood still and thought. 'What about violets? Don't they grow in woodland? There might be some among the trees growing near the lake.'

'Dunno. They might only grow in the spring. But it's worth a try.' I jumped up, gathering my collection into a bag. 'I'll go and look. You coming?'

We went out. The evening was warm and still. Hardly a breeze ruffled the lake. The sun was low, spreading a golden and pink glow behind the hills. We searched for violets but without success. There were some dog roses, and patches of little yellow flowers, but I didn't know their names. I was pretty sure they didn't begin with 'v'. I picked a wild rose, held it in my teeth and pretended to do a Spanish dance.

Chris began:

I suppose
that's just a rose,
but look close
near the water
where you oughta
find the answer, you dancer,
and when you win,
count me in
to share the prize…

I clapped and threw the rose into the mud at the edge of the lake.

'You enjoying yourself here, then?' Chris asked.

I sat down on an uprooted log. Chris sat at the opposite end of it. 'You bet. It's good not to worry about – you know – about what I say and what Mum's thinking, or whether Joe will get himself into trouble without realising.'

'Yeah. You think about Joe too much.'

'What d'you mean?'

'Well, if ever I ask you if you want to swim, or play tennis, or walk the dog, or even just hang out, you always say, "I don't know what Joe's doing," or, "I don't know if Mum wants me to go shopping with Joe," or...'

I stood up, feeling annoyed. 'Well, I have to think about my family.'

'But Joe isn't even your family, and he's an adult, and so's your mum. It's their job. And you are a teenager – nearly – and it's time you had a bit of freedom.'

'I *am* free. I can do what I want. I'm free to do the right thing.'

'You've said it yourself. You don't know what *the right thing* is. Anyway, your family isn't the only one with problems,' he said, his voice rising. 'Tonia...'

'Well if you spent a bit more time with Tonia, you might find out why she's so unhappy.'

'She's eight, and she's a girl! What would I do, spending more time with her? Play dolls' house?' He was scowling.

'You could play tennis with her, then buy her a cola, and sit and drink it with her, and chat to her.'

'Instead of playing tennis with you and chatting with you, you mean?'

'No, I didn't mean...'

'I think I might just do that. Otherwise it's Joe this and Joe that. I'm getting fed up with it.'

'Well, *sorry* if I choose to help my mum sometimes!' I said, sarcastically.

'OK, well, you can look for your own *vile violets*.' He stood up, turned and stalked back in the direction of the hostel.

'Chris, I'm sorry…' I began, but I knew it was too late, and he wouldn't be able to hear me.

'Joe has more understanding in his pinky toe than you've got in your whole body,' I muttered to no one, because now I was *sure* he couldn't hear me. I turned in the opposite direction and walked along the lakeside.

'Don't let the sun go down while you are still angry,' Mum always told me. Too late. The sun had disappeared into the lake, and the crimson sky was fading to mauve. The calm lake stared back at me. I picked up pebbles from the beach and hurled them angrily into the water, shattering the tranquillity, splintering the mirrored reflection of the trees and the darkening sky. Anger had made me feel hot. I slid my arms out of my jacket and hung it on a branch. My walk increased to a jog and I ran through reeds, mud, marsh grass and broken tree stumps, until my feet were soaked and my jeans were caked in mud.

Finally, I stopped and turned inland to stare at the dark trees. There was a lovely smell of damp undergrowth and fresh pine. The woodland in the dusk looked intriguing. I wondered if I might see some nocturnal animals if I waited quietly. Anything to avoid going back to the hostel just yet. I wandered beside the trees and leaned against a trunk, willing my eyes to adjust to the gloom. One tree, in particular, was very inviting. I began to climb it. It was easy, and I climbed quite high. Comfortably astride a branch, I could see the forest floor below me and a glimmer of early moonlight on the lake. I sat, silent and still, looking for badgers and trying to think of *anything* other than Joe or Chris.

After a few minutes, I heard voices approaching. I could just make out two figures, ambling along the edge of the lake, chatting quietly. They stopped where I had stopped, at the point where the mud became thicker. They turned their backs on the woodland and stood looking out over the water, and as they turned, I recognised Ed and Hazel. I took a breath to call out to them, but I realised I should have been back at the house, and I'd probably get told off. After they left, I might be able to sneak back in and pretend I'd been there all along.

'It was awful,' Hazel was saying. 'She was so upset. It was ages before I could get out of her what was wrong.'

'But why didn't she tell her mum – your aunty?' Ed asked. 'Kids are always being told to tell an adult if they're getting bullied.'

I pricked up my ears. Who was being bullied?

'Yeah, but then the bullies threaten worse if you tell. Our family's quite close, and there are seven of us cousins. I'm the oldest, so the others tend to look up to me and tell me things. Miranda especially, because she's the youngest.'

Miranda? Wasn't Tonia's friend called Miranda? But then, there must be other girls called Miranda.

'But what did she say?' Ed asked.

'It wasn't so much what she said, as the way she was acting strangely.'

'What kind of strangely?'

'Oh, things like crying about very little things, and she didn't want to go out to play. Stuff like that.' Hazel picked up a handful of small stones and began skimming them expertly across the water.

'So how did you find out what was wrong?' Ed continued, stroking his chin.

'Miranda had this pencil case. A new sparkly purple one, and I admired it. She said I could have it. Sweet, eh?'

A sparkly purple pencil case? I nearly fell out of the tree. Suddenly I was all ears.

'Let me guess,' Ed said, 'You couldn't bring yourself to tell her you'd grown out of girly stuff?'

'Oh, you never grow out of girly stuff,' Hazel told him. She turned sideways and smiled, and her teeth brace glinted for a moment in the fading light. 'But she said I could have it because she didn't want it. She held it as if it was contaminated, but I didn't take it. Then the fuss started. She cried so hard I couldn't tell what she was trying to say.'

I wanted to climb down and join in with this conversation, but I'd eavesdropped for too long. It was rude, and I felt guilty.

'So how did you guess the problem was bullying?'

'She was being so secretive. D'you remember that visiting speaker we had last year in PSE who told us how to spot signs of bullying? Secrets, change of behaviour and stuff?'

'Go on, Dr Psychologist,' Ed teased.

Hazel pretended to thump him. I realised I'd been holding my breath. I let it out quietly, but then held the next one.

Hazel was continuing, 'She's got a friend at school; well, more like an enemy, really. Tonia, her name is.'

'Tonia? Unusual name. Is it short for something?'

'Dunno. Anyway, Tonia makes Miranda lie for her. Like, say they're playing together when they're not. Stuff like that.'

Tonia!

I craned my neck so as not to miss a word. 'Doesn't sound too serious. Little kids. Little white lies,' Ed said. 'But where does the pencil case come in?'

'I reckon it was a sort of bribe. "Do this for me, and you can have this pencil case" type-thing.'

'Sounds fair enough,' Ed joked. 'D'you think she'd give me a nice present if I told fairy tales for her?'

'C'mon, Ed!' Hazel sounded exasperated. 'Any kind of bullying is serious.' She was speaking more loudly now because she was angry. 'It's not a laughing matter. My little cousin was devastated. If you'd seen her crying…'

'Yeah, yeah. I'm sorry. But what if she'd refused?'

'Well, that's the worst part. Tonia threatens she knows some older boys who she'll tell if Miranda doesn't help her.'

I gasped and Ed looked round for a moment, but then turned back to Hazel.

Older boys? Who did she mean? Not Stuart, or Chris. They wouldn't hurt a fly. Who else did Tonia know?

'Which boys?' Ed demanded.

'Dunno.'

'And Miranda believed her?'

'Seems so. Otherwise she wouldn't have been so upset.'

'Hmm. I get the picture,' Ed said finally, and at last they turned to walk back to the hostel. 'Poor Miranda. What did you say to her?'

'Told her to find some new friends. Told her she must tell an adult – her mum, her teacher, anybody. But she's always been a quiet kid.'

Their voices faded, and I waited a minute or two until I was breathing properly again, then I began to climb down the tree. Climbing down was harder than climbing up, now my legs were full of pins and needles and my feet had gone to sleep completely. I dropped the last two metres and my knees gave way under me. I sat for a few minutes on the sandy, stony ground, not knowing what to think. There must be a misunderstanding. Tonia – a bully? Impossible! But who else did Tonia know? It was so ridiculous I ought to feel amused, but instead I felt angry. But who with?

With Hazel? She'd been trying to cheer up her young cousin.

With Tonia? Chris' feisty little sister? No way!

With Miranda? How can you be angry with someone who got upset?

The feeling was coming back into my feet, making me cringe. Tentatively, I stood up. It was almost dark now, and night rustlings had begun in the woodland and on the hillside. The hidden movements made my scalp prickle, and I wanted to be back inside the warm, light house. So I left the woodland and sloshed along the shoreline, the last of the fading evening light playing on the still water.

In the distance, at the edge of the trees, I saw something moving. There was the flash of a torch. I squatted down and froze, hoping not to be spotted. Where could I go? There was a stretch of open beach between me and the first trees. I held my breath, then heard my name being called. The three figures came nearer. It was Ed, Alison and Lucy, a search party, come to find me. Bother! I sighed and stood up. The others saw me and broke into a jog.

'Hey, Ruth! You OK?' Ed asked.

'Yeah. Course. Just walking. Looking for violets. Something beginning with "v".'

'We thought you were with Chris, but we found him back at the lodge. He said he didn't know where you were.'

'We found your jacket.' Alison held it up. 'You gave us a scare.'

'So you thought I'd been eaten by a bear!' I was trying to joke, hoping I was not in big trouble. I took my jacket.

'Are you OK?' Lucy asked.

I was so surprised by her kindness, I nearly cried. But instead I said, 'Yeah. Course.'

Back at the hostel, Chris was with Ahmed and a couple of others, playing some sort of card game. He saw me come in, and looked away. I left the others downstairs, stuffed my muddy clothes into my bag and climbed into bed. I pretended to be asleep when Alison and Lucy came in soon after, noisily shushing each other.

The next day, our last one at Lochs View, we were divided into two groups. Chris and I were put in different ones. His group would do raft-building in the morning and orienteering in the afternoon. Our group would do the activities the other way round. Chris' group set off straight after breakfast with Hazel, Ed, Mr Bruce and one of the activity leaders from the hostel.

Munro took charge of our group. 'You need brains *and* athletic ability for orienteering,' he said. 'Brains to read a compass and follow a map to lead you to hidden treasure, and speed to arrive back here with all the treasure faster than anyone else. Hands up anyone who has done orienteering before.' We all looked around. A couple of hands went up.

'OK, everyone,' Munro was continuing, 'groups of three. If you can't find two partners, come to me and I'll sort you out.' Lucy and Alison grabbed me. Munro gave each group a map and compass.

'I dinnae ken what to do wi' this,' Lucy grumbled.

Munro must have heard her, and I expected him to tick her off for having a poor attitude, but instead he spread the map on the ground and showed us how to set the compass with the needle pointing north. The other groups crowded round to listen to the explanation. 'Here are your clues. The letters are direction: NW for north-west, and so on. These numbers,' he said, pointing to where he had written them on the map, 'are approximate metres. A metre is roughly the length of your stride if you're running. Set your compass, face the right direction, then count your running steps. The route doesn't go along paths, so you'll have to follow compass directions through the forest, not footpaths or signposts.'

'Mr McAllister, how do *you* know where the buried treasure is?'

'Aha!' he said.

One of the boys sniggered. 'I bet it's because you buried it yourself! Am I right, Mr Munro, sir?'

'Me? Bury treasure? Now, whatever gave you that idea?' Everyone laughed. 'There's enough treasure for everyone, so just take one piece. Don't think you can cheat by taking ten all at once, because they're all different. I'm going to start you at timed intervals. A new group every three minutes. The group that arrives back at base in the shortest time with all ten pieces of treasure might find something to their advantage.'

Our group was sent first. We set the compass. 'North-west, 300 paces,' Alison whispered. 'C'mon.'

'Why are you whispering?' Lucy said.

'Don't want to give the other groups any clues.' She set off at a fast run, counting her paces, and I followed, so Lucy didn't have any choice.

'Shouldn't we have a spade or a trowel or something to dig up the treasure?' I suggested, drawing level with Alison.

She stopped. 'That's 203. Hmm. Never thought about digging.'

'Let's keep going,' I said, 'and see if we can find disturbed earth or something.' We ran on, counting all the time.

'Coming up to 300,' Lucy said, counting and panting. 'Should be somewhere around here. Quick.'

'Thing is,' I said, 'Munro's legs are longer than ours. So his pace must be longer. Maybe we should go a bit further.'

But while I was trying to work it out, Lucy was looking around, kicking at twigs. 'Wait! What's this?' she said. She brushed aside some leaves, and there was a yogurt pot. It was clean, not somebody's litter, and there wasn't any other litter in the wood anyway. Lucy picked up the pot carefully, as if it might bite her, and opened the top. Inside was a handful of blue beads.

'Yes!' we chorused. Lucy took one.

'Let's put it in my pocket,' Alison said. 'My pockets are the deepest.'

'But I found it,' Lucy objected.

'We're a team,' I said. 'Quick, put the pot back and cover it over so the next group doesn't find it straight away.'

Reluctantly, Lucy handed over the bead and replaced the pot.

We followed the next direction and found a red bead, then an oval yellow bead, then a pearly white one, and we began to joke about which of us would have the necklace we made at the end.

'I think I should have it,' Lucy said, 'because I've found most of the pots so far.'

I felt irritated with Lucy, but Alison said, 'C'mon, don't chat. We lose count of our paces if we chat. But anyway, I think Hazel helped Mr McAllister prepare this activity. She probably wants the beads back.'

That was the first time all morning I'd thought of Hazel and the conversation I'd overheard the day before. I'd been enjoying myself. Orienteering was fun. I hadn't even thought of Chris and the argument. I told myself I would apologise to Chris at lunchtime back at the lodge.

In the end, our group wasn't the fastest. We came second, and the first group won a box of chocolates and Munro encouraged them to be *real* heroes and share them out. Alison pulled me aside and whispered, 'D'you think we should invite Lucy to the holiday club at church? Seems like she doesn't have much going for her. Bet she hasn't got any plans for this summer holiday.'

I hesitated. Weeks ago, I would have thought, 'No way!' But I was getting to know Lucy better. She wasn't so bad. And Alison was absolutely right. 'Maybe,' I whispered back.

The raft-building group arrived back at the hostel just after us, and I looked out for Chris, to sit next to him at lunch. They were all wet and laughing and boasting about whose raft was the most successful, when I spotted Chris at the back of the group, walking with Mr Bruce. He was hunched and shivering and whiter than I'd ever seen him.

'Chris – ?' I began, but Mr Bruce held up a hand and called for quiet.

'This lad has hurt his wrist. Needs an X-ray,' he told us, 'just in case it's broken. So I'm going to drive him to the hospital. His mum will pick him up afterwards and take him home.'

There were murmurs of sympathy and some people crowded round Chris and said things like, 'Tough luck,' and, 'Get well soon.'

'Come on, Chris, let's pack your bag and get on the road,' Mr Bruce told him. Chris nodded miserably and trailed after him.

After we got home I texted Chris:

Are you OK?
Yes thanks, he texted back.
What happened?
Badly sprained wrist.
Not broken?
No, but gone black and purple.

That was all. I wondered if I should go to his house and lend him a computer game or something, but his texts were so short, I didn't know if he was still cross with me.

Shall I come and hang out?
Got cousins staying, he texted back.

I took that as a no.

I felt like a terrible friend. I'd quarrelled and not apologised, and now there didn't seem to be any way to chat to him. What's more, I'd never told him about the conversation I'd overheard, and now it seemed so distant and strange, I began to think I'd imagined it, or at least made a big deal of a small thing, since I was feeling so cross and moody at the time.

Anyway, it was time for our annual trip down south to see Nanny and Grandpa Lawrence, my dad's parents. We left Joe on his own in Oliver's flat. Mum said it would be good practice in independent living in Scotland, but I noticed she looked a bit worried as she said it.

'Do you think he might burn the house down or something, Mum?' I asked, half-joking. Then I thought, 'Oops. Bad choice of comment.'

'I think fire is the last thing we might worry about with Joe,' Mum said. 'But I'm just wondering what he'll say if the neighbours ask awkward questions. And I'm a bit worried he'll be lonely.'

But when we arrived at Nanny's house, all Mum's attention was taken up with answering their questions about our life in Edinburgh, her job at the hospital and how I was getting on at school. Nanny and Grandpa were lovely, and always so glad to see us, but I didn't know them very well and I felt they didn't really know me. They kept calling me by one of my cousins' names by mistake. There always seemed to be a kind of quiet sadness about the house, which wasn't surprising, I suppose, since their son, my dad, had died. Grandpa said I looked just like Dad – blonde hair and blue eyes, and something about my chin. His eyes went all misty whenever he said it.

Then, on our second evening there, Cami's WhatsApp message read:

My dad's coming to the UK on business in August. Wish I could come with him.

'Mum,' I said, taking my phone into the kitchen where she was washing up with Nanny. I waited impatiently while she finished what she was saying, then I said, 'Look.' I stuck the phone under her nose so she couldn't miss the message. 'D'you think Cami *could* come? Could she stay with us in Edinburgh while her dad goes to his business meetings? It'd still be school holidays, and we haven't got anything planned after the church holiday club and it'll be my birthday that week.'

Mum didn't answer straight away, which was a very good sign. It showed she was thinking about it.

So began a series of texts, emails and phone calls, resulting in Cami's flight to Edinburgh with her dad being booked for August. And she was coming for a whole week!

15

Mum had been worried about leaving Joe. After we got back from Nanny and Grandpa's, we went round to the flat, and Joe was standing at the front door talking to an old man.

'Ah, hello, Lynn, hello, Ruth,' Joe said. 'This is George, my neighbour.' The old man's face was tanned and whiskery, but his blue eyes twinkled when he smiled.

'Your pal,' George corrected Joe, then stepped forward to offer Mum a brown, leathery hand to shake. 'English language students,' he observed, nodding towards Joe, 'got more time to be sociable than medics. Young Oliver works nights, evenings – I never know when he's around. And now – India!'

'Er… pal?' Joe said.

'Yeah, pal,' George repeated. 'Friend. Those that fish together become pals. Isn't that right, Joe? Friends?'

'Yes. Friends,' Joe said, grinning.

'Fishing?' Mum said. 'You went fishing?' She looked from one to the other.

'Yes,' George said. 'I took this young man down to the Forth with my tackle. Said he used to go fishing as a lad.'

'Did you catch anything?' Mum asked, surprised.

'Oh aye,' George said. 'Brown trout. My missus cooked it for our dinner. Joe came round and shared it with us.'

'*Did* you, Joe?' Mum asked, her eyes wide with amazement.

'Yes. Very good. Taste very good!' Joe beamed with pride.

George turned to Joe. 'Ah, I meant to say. I seen ye working in the garden. Oliver never bothers with it. You're making a good job of it. If you've got time on your hands, in between your studying, like, Mrs Ferguson at number 12 could do wi' some gardening help. She used to pay an old guy to help her, but he got too arthritic. But a strong young guy like you…'

'Oh, yes. Garden. I help. Number 12?'

'That's it. Tell her I sent ye. An' don't refuse payment. She's not short of a penny or two, and you'll embarrass her if you dinnae take it. Students are always in need o' pocket money, I ken. There'll be a couple more neighbours, too, if you're willing.' George turned to me and continued, 'I've seen you and your young friend – Chris, is it? Joe here says you're helping him with his English.'

'Er, yes.' I didn't know what else to say, because I could feel Mum stiffening.

'Aye, that's grand,' George said. He didn't seem to notice that I was tongue-tied. 'Joe says he used to teach maths. In a university.' Mum stared at Joe. This was news to us. Joe looked down, but George didn't seem bothered. He went on, 'I told him, we don't have enough maths teachers here in Scotland. It's what I heard on the radio. Told him he should work hard on his English, then apply for a job.'

Back in our house, Mum was stuffing laundry into the washing machine. She let out a long breath. 'Well!' she said. 'I needn't have worried that Joe would be lonely. He's made a friend, learned a skill and found a way to lend a helping hand. Seems George just thinks he's a language student now. But a maths lecturer? I had no idea.'

'We knew he was good at maths, though,' I said. 'He's always helping me.'

'Yes. Well. But any adult should be able to do S1 maths.'

'But *you* never managed to explain it to me so clearly when I got stuck!'

'Try me at biology. That's my real subject.'

'But Mum! Don't you see? We should've guessed that Joe did something to do with maths, 'cos he always looked carefully and took an interest.'

'Hmm. But you heard what George said. I wonder what else Joe tried to tell him about his past. Or his plans, if he's got any. But it seems his memory is really coming back now.'

'So, is this the moment for him to register? Or give himself up? Or whatever it is you're supposed to do? Surely you've done your job – it's not up to you any more.'

Mum paused, a sock in one hand and a T-shirt in the other. 'It's just that, well, I know that if your dad was here, he'd do everything he could for Joe. I want to do my very best for him as long as he needs help.'

We stared out of the window at the little back garden. It was neat, thanks to Joe. Sometimes, when I knew Mum was missing Dad, I felt quite jealous. I wanted to say, 'But I'm still here! Why do you do things for Dad when he's not even here?' Then I felt horribly guilty. After all, Cami had two parents who loved each other as well as her *and* her brother. And Chris' mum had Daddo.

'But what would happen to you – to *us* – if Joe was found out? Would you go to prison?'

There! I'd said it. It's what I'd been worrying about for ages, but never dared to ask, or even to put into words.

'No, pet!' Mum dropped the laundry and gave me a hug. 'No. I wouldn't go to prison, though I sometimes worry about my job. And *you* won't get into trouble. Don't worry your pretty head.'

'But if you lost your job, what would happen?' Now that I'd started, all the worries seemed to flood out.

'Well, to be honest, pet, I don't know. I really don't know.'

Later, Joe came to our house for dinner. 'This food isn't quite as fresh as the fish you and George caught,' Mum said, smiling.

'George is kind neighbour. Friend,' Joe said.

'Pal,' I supplied. 'Scottish for friend.'

'Joe,' Mum began. 'What did you tell him about… I mean, what do you think he knows…?'

'Don't worry, Lynn,' he said, leaning over to pat her hand. 'I just tell him I staying here while I learning English, and caring for flat while Oliver not here. Then I go.'

'But, Joe, I'm not sure you understand. When you register for asylum, they may send you to a centre – a place to stay – with other asylum seekers. Could be anywhere. Could be England. You won't know anyone.'

'But I *will* know someones. I will know new friends. Pals. I not want to make you and Ruth worry for me. I strong now. Thank you that I strong now.'

'Anyway,' Mum said, her voice light, 'you can't leave us yet. It's the holiday club next week, and we'll need all the help we can get. And the muscle!' She brandished her biceps. Joe grinned.

I knew what Mum was thinking. Getting housed in accommodation far away wasn't the worst of Joe's problems. She was worried that he might be deported, sent to another country, though where would be anyone's guess, since no one seemed to know where he'd come from in the first place – including Joe. Or maybe he *did* know now. He seemed to be remembering more and more all the time.

'Joe,' I began, 'before you came here, to Edinburgh…' But I didn't continue, because Mum was frowning hard at me, and Joe dropped his gaze. He looked down at his hands as he twisted them on his lap.

'I sorry, Ruth. I don't… I can't…'

'It's OK, Joe,' I said quickly. 'I didn't mean to, um, never mind.' I bit my lip.

I wondered if Mum wanted to say, 'I told you so! He still needs help.' But instead, she said brightly, 'There's apple crumble for dessert. Who'd like ice cream with it?'

16

Our church holiday club was called Lighthouse. It took place for a week every summer holiday, but for me it was a first. Mum had agreed to help on Thursday and Friday when she wasn't on shift. Mornings were for primary kids, and evenings for kids at high school, but the leaders said they needed older kids to help with the youngest ones, so I signed up. Mum encouraged Joe to be a helper, too, because they needed plenty of people to move furniture and help to get the room ready.

On the first day we arrived at nine o'clock and prepared the hall. Some of the leaders were people I knew from church, but some were a team who had come specially for the club, and they were staying with local families. The leader was called Greg. He was young – younger than Mum, anyway, and he smiled all the time. His teeth were slightly crooked but it seemed to suit him. He was very energetic and the team obviously loved him. They were all lots of fun. They made every job into a game and we transformed the hall into a seascape, with nets full of plastic fish hanging from the ceiling. There was a cardboard whale and a foam octopus and a length of floaty blue fabric for a wavy sea.

Then we prayed. We asked God to help all the children to understand that Jesus was like a lighthouse, showing where the dangers were, guiding them to a place of safety. Joe stood at the back and watched.

The children arrived at ten o'clock. We wrote down their names on a register and gave them team badges, then took them to craft tables.

Suddenly I spotted a familiar small figure, a girl with dancing dark eyes, a mass of black curls and a springy walk.

'Tonia!' I called, and jumped up to wave. 'Hi, Tonia! Come and help us make boats.' Tonia smiled briefly, then she got busy with the craft straight away.

'Tonia, how's Chris? Is he better?'

'Yeah.'

'What's he doing this holiday?'

'Swimming.'

'Must be a lot better, then,' I thought. I could see Tonia was more interested in making a lolly-stick boat than in talking about her brother, so I didn't ask any more.

Morning by morning we did crafts, played games, sang songs and listened to Bible stories. We made a lighthouse that reached the ceiling. The rocks were cardboard boxes painted grey, and the building was made of huge cardboard tubes that someone's dad had got from work. We painted steps round the outside and windows on the way up. The light at the top was a real, enormous light bulb, rigged up by one of the visiting team members. Rays of light from the lighthouse were made of yellow wool with shimmery gold tinsel, strung all over the hall. When we live in the light, we agreed, we don't tell lies, and we've got nothing to be ashamed of. I glanced at Joe and wondered what he was thinking and how much he could understand, not only of the words, but also of the whole situation.

I kept an eye on Tonia. She seemed to be enjoying herself. There was no sign of the unhappiness that Daddo and Chris had worried about. She joined in with everything and learned the words of the songs really quickly. What had Chris said? She was usually such a 'fun-ball'. Yes. I could see it now. She was so quick and bright and lively, always laughing.

Each morning Greg told a story about someone who met Jesus. Sometimes the team acted the stories, using some of the children as helpers. Sometimes the stories rhymed, or they were made into a quiz or a game. At the end of the story Greg would say a prayer. Sometimes I peeked at Tonia, but she always had her eyes scrunched shut and her hands clasped tightly together.

The last event each morning was team games. There were relay races, ball games and obstacle courses. Someone was needed to demonstrate the obstacle course, and Joe volunteered. He ran round hoops, tossed a beanbag into a bucket, hopped along a mat and finally got stuck under a chair because he was too tall. He clowned around and made everyone laugh. As the race began, he stood nearest Tonia's team. Tonia was small and fast and whizzed round the course and her team won. She turned a couple of cartwheels to celebrate. Joe gave her a high five and she skipped around him in delight. She made a beeline for him each day after that and I could see him talking to her. He was very good at making friends, but I worried about what the friends would ask him.

One day Stuart came to pick Tonia up, and I asked him if Chris was completely better.

'Yep, thanks. He had a badly bruised wrist. They thought it might be broken at first, but it was a bad sprain. Turned all the colours of the rainbow! He even had a sling. Mum had to cut up all his food for him. We had cousins to stay, and that took his mind off it. He's fine now, though. His swimming club's got a gala coming up, so he's training hard and making up for lost time. Then we're going away on holiday.'

Tonia was jiggling up and down, pulling on his hand. 'Gotta go,' Stuart grinned and let her lead him away. As they went, I could see them laughing and chatting together.

The mornings were fun and I was kept busy. Even though I already knew the Bible stories and songs, I never got bored. But the evenings were for older kids and focused on pizza, quizzes, games and discussions, similar to Energise. As Alison had suggested, we invited Lucy. I think she was glad to be invited, though she grumbled when the pizza didn't have any pineapple. For the discussions, we were divided into age groups. There were five in my group – Alison and Daniel, Lucy, me and a boy I hadn't met before, called Paul. I wished I'd invited Chris. Our group leader was Trish. She had green eyes and a ponytail that bobbed up and down when she laughed. She said she was a student and she wanted to be a lawyer.

Each evening after pizza and a few games, we read about someone who met Jesus and we talked about it together. 'Let's shine a light on this story,' Trish always said. She had a yellow tennis ball which she called a light bulb, and threw it to whoever was speaking.

We read the story of Nicodemus, a Jewish teacher of religion, who met Jesus at night and wanted to talk to Him.

Trish shared out the parts for reading: Nicodemus, Jesus and the narrator. Daniel was Jesus, Paul was Nicodemus and Trish asked me to be the narrator. She looked around at everyone. 'Now, we need a beat – a rhythm – like this.' She started to click her fingers. 'Join in.' So we all clicked. 'Now, you readers, can you fit in with the rhythm?'

Suddenly I could see where she was going with it. The whole story was a poem. I cleared my throat, took a deep breath, and began.

Me:
Nicodemus went to visit Jesus in the night.
He didn't want the other priests to see him in the light.
He wasn't sure what Jesus did and said and taught was right,
But didn't want to disagree, to argue or to fight.
He'd seen amazing miracles, like water turned to wine,
And wondered if this really could be something like a sign.

Paul:
We know you are a teacher, Nicodemus said, from God.

But we religious priests are finding what you say quite odd.
It's only with God's help you can do miracles like this.
But is there something else to know – a truth I shouldn't miss?

Daniel:
Jesus answered, 'Nico, you're a teacher – you should know.
You cannot see the wind but you can always hear it blow.
The Spirit is the same, you see, you don't know where He's going,
But miracles and teaching are the Father's way of showing.
You Pharisees don't realise that you must be born again,
And after that you'll understand what God has said and done.'

Me:
So Jesus then explained to those whose minds were dark and closed,
The light would show them up, their evil deeds would be exposed.
But God loves truth and light and sent His Son to show the way
To live the life He plans for us to follow every day.

Trish gave us a clap, then she asked, 'Do you think Nico was a good man or a bad man?'

'Well,' Daniel began. She threw the ball to him. 'Um, he wasn't bad, but he was all about keeping the rules.'

'Boring, huh?'

'Yeah,' Alison said, and Daniel threw the ball to her. 'There's nothing wrong with rules, but he didn't understand that Jesus wanted him to make a new start. To become a friend and follower.'

'Yeah,' said Lucy. 'Jesus talked about light and truth. Not rules.'

'Like a lighthouse,' I agreed. 'To show the way into the safe harbour.'

'Light's good,' Lucy agreed. 'My name means "light".'

Alison and I looked at each other and smiled. I was so glad Alison had suggested inviting her and that I'd finally agreed.

'Thank You,' I prayed silently. 'But what about us? Mum and me? What are we going to do? I can't see how to live in the light while Joe's around.'

17

I loved Lighthouse, but all the time I was counting the days till Cami arrived. I was sorry she wouldn't be coming in time to join in, but at least we would have every day to ourselves, and we'd be able to choose what to do.

Slowly, I had been making friends at school. There was Alison and Daniel and Lucy and a couple of other girls in my class, and, of course, there was Chris. But old friends, like Cami, were still the best.

One evening, Mum let me phone her for a chat. But before I phoned, I asked Mum, 'Have *you* made any new friends here?'

She frowned and thought for a minute.

'Is Joe your friend?' I continued.

She smiled. 'I guess he's an *old* friend, but not like Cami. I think he's, well, he's a sort of project. One day, he'll be strong and independent, but I want to give him the best start I can. Or the best start *we* can.'

I felt proud to be part of the project, and relieved to hear that Mum expected Joe to get completely better. Then I phoned Cami.

'Hey, Ruthie!' she squeaked. 'I can't wait! There's so much I want to hear about. And tell you.'

'Yeah. Me too. There's one very important thing, though. We've got a family friend who Mum used to know in Damascus, who often comes to eat with us.'

'Oh? Who is she?'

'He. It's a man. He's called Joe. We think he's from Palestine. He was living in Syria, but he had to escape when the civil war started. He was quite injured.'

'Oh, how awful! Is he better now? Is he going to stay in Scotland, or does he want to go home?'

'Well, the thing is, he doesn't have a home. So, yes. He's staying here. At least for the moment.'

'Ah.'

'He worked with my dad – a long time ago. At the hospital in Damascus.'

I knew I was avoiding telling the whole truth, even though she was my best friend. I wasn't living in the light, but not in the darkness, either. Maybe in the shadow. At least now she wouldn't be taken by surprise.

I thought it best to change the subject. 'What was it you were going to tell me?'

'Oh, just – I won an art competition.'

'Oh, well done, Cami! What's the prize?'

'I'm going to have my painting displayed in an art gallery in central Cairo. I might even be able to sell it, but Mum says she wants to keep it forever.'

And so I avoided having to explain a load of stuff about Joe, but just said enough before Cami actually met him.

Mum and I went to the airport to meet Cami and her dad. I was worried that I might not recognise her. It had only been five months since we had been together, but a lot can happen in that time. A lot *had* happened. I wondered if there was anything more in *her* life that she hadn't told *me*. Did she have any dark secrets, or was she living in the light? I looked at myself in the mirror. Had I changed? Would *she* recognise *me*? Instead of grabbing the nearest jeans and T-shirt in my wardrobe, I stood and thought about what to wear. Did Cami have fashionable clothes? I remembered how we didn't used to bother, but she was thirteen, now, and she had new friends, just as I had. I chose some denim cut-offs and a turquoise top with shimmery bits round the neck. I took a navy jacket, too, in case it got chilly.

I looked at the electronic arrivals board. There were so many planes. They came from Barcelona, Amsterdam, Venice, Paphos, Lanzarote, Frankfurt and dozens of places I'd never heard of.

'But there's nothing from Cairo,' I said, feeling panicky.

'They're coming via Amsterdam,' Mum reminded me. 'We always had to go via another airport, remember? Usually Istanbul, or sometimes Heathrow.'

'Look,' I squeaked. 'There they are!'

Cami had been trudging along behind her dad, pulling her suitcase, but as soon as she saw me, she jumped up and down and waved like mad. I ran to the barrier and hopped from foot to foot until they came through. Then we hugged and squealed and she was just the same old Cami. She might've been a bit taller, but her hair was still long and curly and I even recognised her favourite flowery T-shirt. We skipped off together towards the exit, leaving Mum to greet Cami's dad and to pick up her suitcase.

Finally, we stopped, of course, while her dad gave her a hug and all sorts of warnings and instructions to be helpful and polite and not to get in the way. Mum laughed and said she was looking forward to having extra help with the chores. They arranged when and where he would pick Cami up when he had finished his business meetings and it was time to fly back to Cairo, but meanwhile, we had a whole week together.

'What would you like to do? And what do you want to see?'

'Well, I don't know anything about Edinburgh, so it's up to you.'

'Edinburgh's great! There's so many parks and the castle and Princes Street Gardens and the Royal Commonwealth Pool and…'

Cami was laughing. 'What?' I demanded.

'You sound like your mum when she was trying to persuade you that Edinburgh's a good place.'

'Oh. Well. She was right.' And I laughed, too.

We carried Cami's suitcase up to my room, where Mum had made up a bed for her on a mattress on the floor. She liked our house and, like me, she stood at my window and looked at the hills. 'It's so green,' she said.

'I know. Different, eh?'

There was so much to talk about, but we had all week. Mum called us down for dinner. She had made a delicious casserole called Moroccan Lamb, served with couscous. She'd deliberately chosen a Middle Eastern dish to make Cami feel at home. 'I've invited Joe, too, 'cos I'm sure it'll be familiar to him.'

Joe arrived looking very smart, in pressed jeans and a crisp shirt and with his hair neatly combed.

Mum said, 'Joe, we'd like you to meet Camilla – Cami.'

'Hello,' Cami said, holding out her hand to shake.

Joe shook her hand and gave her a little bow. '*Enchanté*,' he said, like in an old film. Cami giggled and blushed.

'Joe!' I said, 'Where did you…?'

But Mum continued, 'Cami is Ruth's very best friend from Cairo.'

'I know,' said Joe.

'But Joe, you've never…' I began.

'I know she is best friend. Ruth talk every day of Cami.'

'Yeah, well,' I said, and Cami and I smiled at each other. She was still the same Cami and I hoped I was still the same Ruth. Sisters always.

We talked about Cami's journey and her family, and her school and my school. Joe joined in, chatting and asking questions. Mum made us laugh, telling us about one of her patients who encouraged everyone on the ward to sing 'O Flower of Scotland' one day when the Scottish football team won a match. The ward sister tried to shush him, but all the patients knew the song and most people joined in, and everyone was more friendly after that. Joe was watching Mum as she spoke, and then he began to sing the song himself.

'We taught him that,' I said. 'Chris and me.'

At the mention of Chris, everyone was quiet for a moment. Then Mum said, 'We haven't seen him for ages. What's he been up to this holiday?'

'After he hurt his wrist on the Venture, his cousins came to stay. Then after his wrist was better, he had a swimming gala to train for, then he went away with his family,' I said quickly. I still felt bad because I hadn't apologised. I hadn't told Mum anything about our argument, either.

'C'mon,' I said to Cami. 'Let's go upstairs. Er, Mum, do we have to do the…?'

'No washing-up tonight,' she said, laughing. 'I'll do it and I expect Joe will help me. You girls have a lot to catch up on.'

In my room we sat on Cami's mattress on the floor and I told her about the Venture, including the quarrel I'd had with Chris before he was injured. I described how I'd stalked off and climbed a tree and overheard Hazel and Jamie talking about Tonia. 'But Tonia's fine now,' I said, and then I told her about Lighthouse and about how Lucy and Tonia had both enjoyed it.

Cami listened carefully, only stopping me occasionally to ask a question. It was such a relief to tell someone after all this time.

We went to bed soon after that, but I lay awake for ages, and I thought about the last time Cami had come to stay, in Cairo, when the crazy wind had blown away our old life. Cami was asleep. I could tell by her breathing. But I lay and thought how I could say sorry to Chris and make sure we were still friends.

18

'What about your birthday?' Mum asked at the beginning of the week. 'Do you want to have a party?'

I pulled a face. 'I don't have enough friends to invite. Anyway, Cami's here. She's enough for a party. Cami as guest of honour, then pizza for dinner.' Cami laughed and hugged me.

'OK,' Mum said, 'but how about inviting Chris, too?'

'Oh, I dunno.'

'Just for pizza?'

'Go on,' Cami urged. 'I want to see what he's like.'

'Tell you what,' Mum said. 'Why not invite his little sister as well, since we know her from Lighthouse?'

'And what about the twins you told me about – you know – the ones from Energise?' Cami added.

'Alison and Daniel. Yeah. Good idea.'

'And Lucy?' Mum suggested. 'I met her mum at the parents' evening. And she came to Lighthouse, didn't she? I reckon she'd be pleased to be invited.'

'I guess so,' I replied, trying not to sound reluctant. So I phoned round and everyone said they'd come. But meanwhile, Cami and I had a week to spend together.

We had a wonderful time. I had saved up as much pocket money as I could, which wasn't all that much, but Cami's dad had given her a heap of extra money. I laughed when she couldn't count it properly and didn't know if things were expensive or not.

'It's not my fault,' she protested. 'You know we don't use pounds and pence in Egypt.' It was true. I remembered I'd had trouble with the money when we first arrived, but I'd gone everywhere with Mum, and she'd paid.

Cami and I visited the castle, and we loved the prison where you could hear the prisoners whispering in the dark. We knew it was only a recording, but it made us shiver. Cami liked the pet cemetery, and we both stood with our fingers in our ears watching a soldier fire the one o'clock gun. I told Cami about Joe thinking the one o'clock gun was a terrorist attack.

We went to Cramond, and I told her about the Somerfield gang and about Joe juggling. This time we arrived just as the tide was going out, so we walked to Cramond Island and back without getting stranded there.

One day it rained, so we went swimming, not at the Royal Commonwealth Pool, but at our smaller local pool, but it wasn't too crowded. We went to the nearby shopping centre, but Cami said the shops were ordinary and she wanted to see real Scottish shops, so we went to the Royal Mile instead and she bought a tartan purse for her mum and a cuddly Loch Ness monster for Alexander. Then I told her about the conversation on my first day at school at break time, and how I'd pretended I had a boyfriend called Alexander. 'Don't ever tell him,' I begged. She giggled and promised.

Mum drove us to the bottom of Arthur's Seat and we walked to the top. 'Who was Arthur?' Cami asked.

'No one really seems to know, but it's the shape of the hill – a seat and a back.' We could see the whole city from up there. 'This is really just the Queen's back garden,' I said. It was what Chris had told me. 'Look, there's Holyrood Palace, where she stays when she visits Edinburgh. And that's the Scottish Parliament building.' I pointed.

'Looks like a boat,' Cami said.

'Yeah. Several boats. Scotland's very good for fishing.'

When my birthday arrived, Cami gave me a lovely red blouse made of Egyptian cotton, with a Middle Eastern design of peacocks and exotic flowers. She'd kept it secretly in her suitcase ever since she'd arrived. I unwrapped it at breakfast time with Mum there, so she could see it, too. I loved it, and gave Cami a big hug. Mum gave me a whole bag of parcels, but the most special one was a stunt kite.

'What?' Cami asked, her eyes wide.

'You know how windy it can be in Edinburgh?' I said. She nodded. 'And you know how many big parks we've got? Well, I've seen kids with stunt kites and it looks like a lot of fun.'

'I'm jealous,' Cami said, grinning. 'We wouldn't have that sort of space anywhere in Cairo.'

'Nor that sort of wind,' I added.

'Except for that night!' Mum said, and we three remembered that night when Cami had stayed over.

Later in the morning, Joe came round with a little pink envelope, which he handed to me. I opened it carefully. It contained a tiny silver chain with a little swirly Celtic design pendant. It was very pretty and delicate. I looked at Joe and then at Mum. She nodded and I hugged him for the first time. He hesitated, then hugged me back. He gave me a huge grin and his face and neck went quite pink. I think he was pleased that I was pleased.

'He chose it himself,' Mum said.

'It's beautiful. Thank you, Joe,' I said, and put it on straight away.

At five o'clock Joe came round again and Chris, Tonia, Lucy, Alison and Daniel arrived. I thought Chris and I would feel awkward, but I think having all of us there helped. The twins gave me an umbrella that you could fold up really small. 'Just to remind you you're not in Egypt any more,' Alison said, 'and it rains almost every day here.'

Lucy gave me a pink T-shirt with *Proud to be a Scot* on it. 'Me and Alison decided to make you into a real Scottish girl!' she said with a grin.

Chris handed me an envelope, but he didn't really look at me. I assumed it was a birthday card, but he and Tonia stood still and watched while I opened it. It was a voucher for a couple of sessions at a local climbing wall.

'Oh, wow! I love climbing.'

Chris looked at me, then, with a half-smile, and I knew he was thinking about the first time I went to his house and climbed in through his window. It was our secret.

We had Mum's homemade pizza followed by many flavours of ice cream and a birthday cake with thirteen candles. I'd told Mum I was too old for a cake with candles, but she'd insisted, so Tonia and I blew them out while everyone sang 'Happy Birthday' and cheered and clapped.

When we'd all eaten as much as we could, we sat back and Daniel said, 'When Alison and I were small we used to have an entertainer – like a conjuror or something – to our birthday parties. Can anyone do card tricks?' He looked around.

'I know!' I said suddenly. 'Joe can juggle. Show us some juggling tricks, please, Joe?'

I managed to find three tennis balls and Joe juggled, just as he had done on Cramond Beach.

Mum watched in amazement. Joe just smiled. Cami asked to try, so Joe took us all outside and gave us a few lessons. When we went back inside, Mum said, 'Now, who else can entertain us?'

They stayed all evening, and when they left to go home, Chris said quietly, 'Thanks. I'm glad you invited me.'

'I'm glad you came,' I said, and we shared a proper smile.

After they'd gone, Mum pulled me into a hug. 'Well, honey?'

'It's funny, Mum, but I think that was one of the best birthdays I've ever had, even though we arranged it at the last minute.'

'Chris is nice,' Cami said later as we got ready for bed. 'He seems like a good friend. And your mum says it's thanks to you and him that Joe speaks such good English. But he and Tonia don't look at all alike.'

So I explained about Daddo and how Chris and Stuart's surname was Miller but Tonia's was Agard. 'Yeah. He *is* nice. Maybe we'll go back to normal once school starts again. I really want to find a chance to say sorry. I don't want the argument to stop us being friends.'

19

After Cami left, I felt terrible. It was just like when we first came back to Scotland and I missed Cami so much and I didn't know what to do and didn't have anyone to do it with. Mum thought I'd feel better once we were back at school, but I wasn't looking forward to it.

Me to Cami: *Missing you horribly. Come back.*
Cami to me: *Me too. Wish I could.*

The only good thing about the new term beginning was that Energise began again as well, after a summer break. Lucy came, and this time I plucked up the courage to invite Chris. He already knew Daniel and Alison, and probably some of the others. Maybe I'd get a chance to apologise.

The introductory game involved drawing. Aimee had written activities, such as 'playing football', 'watching TV' and 'painting' on cards. We had to take a card and draw the activity, without speaking, so that our team could guess it. When it was my turn, I had to draw someone fishing. I'm hopeless at drawing, but Chris guessed it correctly. When it was his turn, he drew someone cooking, and I got it. We grinned at each other. 'Great minds think alike,' I thought.

Pizza was delivered, and Lucy didn't complain about the lack of pineapple. We sat at a table with Daniel and Alison. They'd spent the last week of the school holiday on the Isle of Skye and the weather had been good, so they were very tanned. 'We were camping, so we were outside all the time,' Alison said.

'But in the evenings, there were swarms of midges, so we had to cover ourselves up,' Daniel said.

'Those midges really loved Daniel,' Alison told us. 'He got so bitten, and he was so itchy, he developed a new dance.' She stood up to demonstrate Daniel jiggling about with itchy midge bites, and Chris and Lucy laughed, but I remembered mosquito bites from Egypt and felt sorry for him.

It was Question Box time and Nathan chose one of the boys to pick a card.

He read, 'What do you think of truth?'

'You're supposed to tell it.'

'And not tell lies.'

'Is it *always* wrong to tell lies?' Aimee asked.

'Not if you do it so as not to hurt someone's feelings,' one of the girls suggested.

'Like what?'

'Like – what do you think of my new jacket? And you think it's awful but you say it's nice.'

'What do you all think?' Nathan asked.

Some people agreed, others disagreed. Alison suggested you could say something true, but not really answer the question, like, 'It's a nice colour.'

'If you don't tell the truth, you're not living in the light,' said Lucy. 'At Lighthouse, they said we should live like there was a light shining on what we did. No shadows. When you tell lies, you end up having to tell more lies, then you forget what you've said, and…'

'And the dark gets darker, eh?' Nathan said.

'Yeah.'

'Isn't "the truth" one of the names Jesus called Himself?' Daniel asked. '"The way, the truth, and the life"?'

'But wouldn't all the other religions say that *they* have the truth?' Chris queried.

'Yes, they probably would,' Nathan agreed. 'But Jesus also said, "Seek, and you will find," and I believe that if we really want to know the truth, we will find it.'

We stacked up the chairs and played obstacle races. Nathan had made it really funny. It involved not only running and dodging and throwing balls into buckets, but also standing on a chair and reciting a nursery rhyme or singing a song, doing a dance in a hoop and spelling your best friend's name backwards. In the end, we were laughing so much, we never found out which team won.

The evening finished with a game of basketball. Aimee had promised Alison and Daniel. Chris enjoyed himself. 'Don't know why I didn't come before,' he said as we said cheerio to Nathan and Aimee and filed out of the door. I felt ashamed, because the reason was probably that I hadn't invited him. But I was glad he'd enjoyed it.

Mum hadn't yet arrived to pick me up, so I sat on the wall to wait, and Chris said he'd wait with me.

'Chris,' I began, 'at the Venture…'

'I know,' he said. 'I'm sorry for saying what I did about Joe. You and your mum have done a fantastic job looking after him. When he *does* finally apply for asylum, he'll be able to cope with English and everything.'

'But the argument was my fault,' I said, looking away. 'I should have listened when you were worried about Tonia. I shouldn't have gone off in a huff like that. I'm sorry.'

We sat silently for a moment, gazing down the street. Then I turned to face him. 'Friends?' I asked.

'You bet!' He grinned and gave me a high five.

'Anyway, Joe's so much better, he's already talking about registering for refugee status. Then he'd be legal. *If* they accept his case. Mum's still worried about him. She wants him to wait a bit longer, so she says we should still keep quiet. It's hard – like trying *not* to tell the truth.'

'Yeah.' We sat in silence for a minute, then Chris added, 'Showing him round gave me some ideas for my project, though. Gave us some laughs.'

We laughed again as we remembered 'playing haggis', and suddenly a figure appeared from the pathway that ran alongside the church.

Adam Somerfield!

'Well, well. You two still together?' He looked at me. 'How's your mum, and her *friend*? New boyfriend, is he?'

Horrified, I took a breath to object, but Chris stood up quickly. 'Somerfield! No big brother to protect you today, then?'

'Some big brothers are good pals. Others are useless!' He carried on walking, chuckling to himself.

I took a deep breath. 'D'you think he overheard us? What do you think he meant? About my mum?'

'Oh, don't take any notice of him. He might have seen your mum with Joe and assumed he was her boyfriend.'

'But it's not like that,' I began.

'Don't worry. He doesn't know anything. He was just being annoying. He'll forget about it.'

'And what did he mean about big brothers? And about being useless?' I chewed my lip and thought about it.

Chris had gone quiet. Then he said, 'I think he meant me. I'm a pretty useless brother sometimes. Like you said.'

'Oh, but I didn't mean…' I began, remembering what I'd said at the Venture, about him not listening to Tonia. 'I'm sorry.'

'It's OK.' We stared down the road, then Chris said, 'Remember our agreement to take Joe to see the Festival Parade?'

'Er, yeah. D'you still want to?'

'Of course. If you do.'

So we agreed.

20

'Good job we came early,' Chris commented. He and Joe and I took our places among thousands of others lining Princes Street, ready for the Festival Parade. It was impossible to talk and hear each other. We had to shout above the noise of the excited crowd. I'd feared the long wait might be boring, but there were so many candyfloss sellers, clowns on stilts and characters in fancy dress, advertising everything from hot dogs to bungee jumps, that even waiting was entertaining.

When a pipe band heralded the first float, the crowd pushed up to the barrier and seemed to grow taller. We craned our necks as float after float and band after band paraded past, advertising their show, giving all the spectators a foretaste of the fun and fascination of the festival.

Bagpipe music, Korean drums, a brass band and a Slovenian choir mingled to a cacophony of noise, constantly moving, flowing forwards, while thousands of performers smiled, waved, danced, acted, sang, shouted and advertised their event.

A pantomime cow drew laughs from the small children while, beside it, a Chinese dragon wove its colourful way from side to side, shaking its magnificent head. Shakespearean actors, classical musicians, comedians, acrobats, magicians and cheerleaders all competed for everyone's attention.

'Look, Joe! Jugglers. You could do that,' Chris said, as a team of sequinned Chinese performers dazzled us all with their feats. There were international youth orchestras, amateur dance groups, monocyclists and one-man bands shouting the number of their venue and handing out flyers.

We three kept hold of each other in case we got separated in the shifting crowd. Eventually, the spectators began to thin out as the last stragglers brought up the rear of the parade. 'Let's go and see if there are any Fringe events or street performers who've already started,' Chris urged.

'Why do they call it the Fringe?' I asked, as we crossed to the wide, paved area beside the art galleries at the foot of the steep road leading up to the castle.

'I suppose it's because it happens *round the edge* of the main festival,' Chris suggested. 'Anyway, the Fringe events are much cheaper than the main festival events, and some of them are free.'

Colourful market stalls had been set up on the open paved area overlooking the gardens, selling Peruvian hats, Indian cotton skirts with shimmery mirrored hems, bright silver-coloured jewellery and exotic dried fruits. Artists sketched portraits, hair-braiders braided hair and a young guy with too many facial piercings to count painted henna tattoos on bare arms or legs.

Suddenly, I felt Chris' grip tighten on my arm. 'Look! A fire-eater. I think we should steer Joe away.' It was too late. Joe stood still at the back of the crowd, and folded his arms across his chest. 'What do you think he's thinking?' Chris hissed.

'Dunno. He's been so much better recently, so much more confident. And his English is brilliant. He's so funny, sometimes, too. He makes Mum and me laugh. I think we should move on, though. Hang on, that's my phone.'

It was Mum. She wanted to meet us on the Royal Mile, outside the Festival Fringe office.

Chris went over to Joe. 'Let's move on,' he said.

'Yes,' Joe replied, frowning. 'Fire. It is not for play. Not a toy. Some people, they are crazy. They think always about fire.'

'I know,' Chris agreed. He turned to me. 'Like Adam and his project.' Then he added, 'It's like some people have got a bee in their bonnet about fire.' Joe looked blank. 'A bee in their bonnet,' Chris repeated. He mimed a bee buzzing round his head. 'Crazy.'

'Yes,' Joe agreed. 'You. You are crazy!'

I was happy, because we were all getting on so well, as if the argument had never happened. 'Come on, let's go up The Playfair Steps,' I told them. 'I'll race you.' And I ran, darting in and out of the festival visitors strolling in the sunshine, and up the long, long flight of steps.

Chris accepted the challenge and raced up the steps two at a time.

'You two, you are crazy and too slow!' came Joe's voice, panting, as he overtook us both, taking the steps in threes. I remembered for a moment how weak and sick he had been in the spring. We arrived at the top, gasping and laughing, leaning on the railings to get our breath back. From there we could see most of Princes Street, and groups of people dispersing in all directions, while other groups stood around, hoping for more action.

Eventually, we took the last part of the walk more slowly, and paused to stand on the Royal Mile. We looked uphill towards the castle, and downhill towards Holyrood Palace. 'Up there,' I pointed. 'There's the Fringe Office, with the harlequin statue outside.'

Mum was already there, and the three of us told her about the varied music, the energetic activity and the vibrant colours of the parade.

'Sounds great,' she said, smiling warmly. 'There's a free concert at St Giles' Cathedral at the moment. I saw the notice as I walked by. Let's go and see.'

'Mum,' I began, glancing at Chris. Who would want to go into a dark building on a lovely sunny day? But then I saw the poster advertising the event. It was a Palestinian lute player. I looked at Chris and pointed my chin towards the poster. He nodded, understanding.

Anyone was allowed to wander quietly around the cathedral, and the area where the musician was tuning up had been divided off. He began to play, and the lilting music echoed round the vaulted ceiling of the cathedral.

Joe and Mum sat down near the back to listen and I sat beside them, while Chris went to look at a little stall that sold postcards and guide books.

After a minute or two, I felt Joe stiffen. I turned to look at him. His eyes were wide, his jaw set. Mum had turned, too. 'What is it?' she whispered.

'My language!' Joe said. 'He sing my language!'

'Oh, lovely!' Mum smiled, but Joe's expression was dark. His fists were clenched and he glowered at the singer.

'What is it, Joe?' I asked. 'What's the matter?'

'He sing very bad things. Like – not true. He sing of free… freeness.'

'Freedom.'

'He sing of freedom. But there is no freedom in my country.' His voice had risen, and people were glancing in our direction.

'Time to go,' Mum mouthed to me. We stood up, and Chris moved to join us.

'Not such a good idea,' I muttered to him. 'Tell you outside.'

'Always same problem,' Joe said, as we stepped out into the sunshine. 'In my country, they talk, they write, they sing, they dream of freedom. But people hurt, they kill, they close in prison.'

'But freedom is a good aim,' Mum argued. 'If people hold on to their dream of freedom in the future, and work for it, maybe it will become reality, like it is here in the UK.'

'Yes, here is very good, but for you. Here you are free. You can say truth. But here is not for me. Here is not my place. I wait, but I think I must go.'

'But not yet,' Mum pleaded. 'Wait till you're really strong, then apply for refugee status.' She had turned to face him, and the two of them stood, talking earnestly. People began to give them a wide berth, until they were in a little oasis of space, with life going on unnoticed around them.

'Look, a monocyclist!' Chris said, pulling me over to watch a street performer drumming up support. I could tell Chris was embarrassed by the argument, and he pretended to give his rapt attention to the performer. But it was impossible to ignore Joe and Mum. We could still hear almost all their conversation, despite the chattering around us, and the laughter and applause of the gathering crowd.

'If you wait until you can speak English perfectly, you'll find it easier to get a job,' Mum was saying. 'You could write a good application. You could use your maths. The authorities would see what an asset you'd be to the community.'

'You are very kind,' Joe said. 'You and Ruth. But I am not good for you. I make danger for you.'

'Not as much danger as you would if…'

'But you don't like lies. I know. You and your daughter. You are women of faith. Not tell lies. You have good heart. Lies very bad for you. Give you bad heart.' Joe thumped his chest with his fist. 'I want to live in the light. Like you. But I give you bad heart.'

I gripped Chris' arm. His gaze was fixed on the cyclist, but I knew that, like me, he was taking in every word.

With the crowd of spectators pressing in around us to watch the juggler, and the anxiety of Joe and Mum's conversation, I felt trapped. I wanted to get away. Slowly, I turned my head to work out my escape route. Then I saw, quick as a flash, a hand slipping into Chris' jeans pocket to steal his mobile phone. The owner of the hand melted backwards away from the crowd and began to walk briskly downhill. Just as quickly, I pulled away from Chris and elbowed my way through the crowd with murmurs of 'Sorry. 'Scuse me!'

The pickpocket glanced over his shoulder and broke into a run.

'Hey!' I shouted, and lunged, tackling him around the knees and bringing him down heavily on the pavement. He dropped Chris' phone as he fell, and it went skittering along the cobbles. In the struggle, Joe was suddenly there, pinning the thief by the shoulders. I got a good look at the boy for the first time. He was young, not much older than us, but smaller and lighter than Chris. I stood up and rubbed my knee.

'OK, love?' Mum asked anxiously.

'My phone!' Chris exclaimed, picking it up and checking it. The boy's eyes darted from one to the other of us. He looked terrified.

'You very bad!' Joe scolded mildly. 'Now go!' Joe let the boy stand up. He didn't need to be told twice. He sprinted away and was soon lost among the milling groups of people. The onlookers, no longer interested in my rugby tackle, quickly transferred their attention back to the street monocyclist.

'You are very skilful,' Joe praised me. 'Very fast and strong. Like playing haggis!'

'You shouldn't have let him go,' Chris complained to Joe. 'We should've called the police.'

'No way,' Mum shuddered. 'All those questions!'

I understood what she meant, but wondered if the thief would be more successful next time. What if he'd been a mugger, not just a pickpocket? How much longer could this hiding game continue?

Me to Cami: *Went to Festival Parade. Caught a pickpocket.*
Cami to me: *What? You a heroine now?*

21

Mum said it was a pity that schools went back while the festival was still on, because it meant Scottish schoolkids had to miss such a lot. She took Joe to a couple of lunchtime shows when she wasn't working, but there was one that started at five o'clock in a hall just off the Grassmarket. It was Highland dancing. She said I'd enjoy it, and I thought I probably would, but it meant leaving school the moment the final bell sounded and dashing out to meet her and Joe at the end of the road. We drove into town, then took ages trying to find a parking space. When we did, it was miles away, and Mum grumbled that it cost almost as much as the festival tickets.

We had to run in order not to be late, but once we got there, we did enjoy it. The troop looked great – the men in their kilts and the girls in white dresses with tartan sashes over one shoulder. They were so light on their feet you could hardly hear them. They managed to be energetic but graceful at the same time. There was a ceilidh band, with an accordion player, a bassist, several violins and a drummer. It made me want to join a dance troop. I reckoned I could pick it up quite easily.

At the end, the audience spilled out into the street. The sun was dazzling and it made us squint. When I could open my eyes properly, someone was dashing across the road towards us.

'Hey! I've been waiting for you for ages.'

'Chris! What's wrong? What are you doing here? Has something happened?'

Mum and Joe had stopped. We were all standing still, watching Chris jiggle from foot to foot while the festival crowds surged around us. 'I knew you were coming to a show after school. In our class, we had to present our projects today. I had to do mine first. Then...'

'Oh, how did it go?' I interrupted.

'OK. But listen. At the end, Adam Somerfield told Mr Bruce and the whole class where I'd got my information from.' He looked at Joe.

'But Chris, you promised,' I wailed.

'I didn't say a thing. Honestly. Not a thing.' He looked near to tears.

'What did Adam Somerfield say?'

'He said my friend and her mum were harbouring a guy who was here in Scotland illegally. Said you were hiding him from the police. Said he'd go to prison if he got found out.'

'Hang on, Chris,' Mum said. 'I don't understand.' She looked at her watch. 'But can we walk as we talk? The parking metre's about to run out and I don't want to pay a fine.' She told him where we'd left the car. 'Tell me as we go. D'you need a lift?'

She walked briskly and we all followed, while Chris continued breathlessly, 'I'm so sorry. I never told anyone about Joe. Not my parents. Not even Stuart or Tonia. They just think he's a family friend, not that he's – you know – illegal. But somehow, Adam found out that we were trying not to say anything.'

I suddenly remembered how Adam had appeared out of nowhere when Chris and I were sitting on the wall at the end of Energise. What did he overhear? What had we said? I know that was when we each apologised, and I'd felt so much better afterwards. But what else had we said? Was there something about Joe? Then I knew Joe himself had talked to Tonia at Lighthouse. What had he said? I couldn't think properly.

We were all trying to walk briskly, single file, through the narrow backstreets, and hear each other at the same time. 'Mr Bruce said he wanted to have a word with me after class, but I just bolted out as soon as the bell went and came straight here to warn you. But…'

'Thanks, Chris,' Mum said. 'I guess it had to happen. Sounds like it wasn't your fault. I don't know what's going to happen now.'

I could see Chris hadn't finished. He was jogging, out of breath, trying to say something. He went on, 'But while I was waiting, Mum phoned. She said Tonia has gone missing. Tonia had told Mum she was going round to Miranda's, then Mum saw Miranda and her mother at the supermarket and Tonia wasn't with them. Miranda's mum said they hadn't seen Tonia for ages.'

Mum stood still and we all bumped into each other. 'Oh, my goodness! Well, we'd better all get home as fast as we can. Come on.'

We all began to jog. 'This way's better, Lynn. It's a short cut,' Chris said, and turned sharply left up a small alley, the sort I wouldn't take at night, but a boy, head down, running at full tilt, collided with me and knocked me into Joe.

'Slowly, slowly,' Joe said, catching hold of me so I could get my balance. He grabbed the boy's arm. The boy looked up. His grubby face was streaked with tears. It was Adam Somerfield.

He looked round and spotted Chris. 'Sorry, Miller. So sorry.'

'You shouldn't have…' Chris began, but Adam was hiccupping and pointing. 'Your sister…' he sobbed, and broke free of Joe's grip and sprinted away down the alley.

Chris looked in the direction Adam had pointed. A tiny puff of smoke drifted above the old rooftops. Chris began to run. We all followed.

He stopped on a corner beside a small grocer's shop with a 'Closed' sign on the door. Metal grid shutters covered the windows. We all looked up at a small, high, side window. A thin wisp of smoke curled from it. Chris ran up to the front of the shop and tried to squint through the mesh, shading his face with one hand to get a better view. 'There's someone in there!' he gasped. 'I can't see anything, but I can hear a voice.'

Someone began beating on the door from the inside, rattling the handle. Then we heard a thin, high wail.

We all seemed to freeze for a moment, then Chris yelled, 'Tonia! What're you…? Tonia! The door's locked.' Joe elbowed Chris out of the way and shook the door handle, put his shoulder to it and pushed, then kicked it with all his strength, like they do on TV, but it was no use.

'Other side,' Joe said, and we all ran round the corner.

Mum was on her phone. 'Fire and ambulance,' I heard her say.

There was a window with frosted glass. Joe pulled his sleeve over his hand and punched the glass in. With the rush of air came a loud crack and a burst of flame. Black smoke gushed from the shop into the little room and billowed out of the broken window. It was a store room. Through the smoke I could just see piles of boxes.

'Back, back,' Joe shouted, pushing me away, and despite Mum's screams he scrambled through the window.

Doors started to open across the road. A woman appeared, carrying a bucket of water. She was about to throw it into the window, but I shouted, 'Wait!' I pulled my gym T-shirt out of my bag and plunged it into the water. I balled it up and roared, 'Joe! Wet cloth!' and hurled it in through the window. I could just make out its white shape as Joe wrapped it round his head. Then, ramming his shoulder against the door into the shop, Joe broke the lock. I heard the door give way with a splintering crunch as he burst into the room. I was so scared I could hardly breathe.

Mum yelled to Joe, 'Keep your head down! Breathe through the cloth!' Above the crackling and spitting, Mum's shouts and my own sobs, I could hear the wonderfully welcome sound of a siren. Help was coming!

There was a flash of white and Joe reappeared, coughing, struggling, carrying something – or someone. 'Lynn! Chris! Ruth! Please to help!' he gasped. Slipping out of his jacket, Chris bundled it over the broken glass at the bottom of the window frame, while Joe lifted Tonia over the sill. Chris and I reached out to take her from Joe while Mum helped Joe to climb out.

Tonia seemed to be unconscious. Chris carried her while I supported her head.

We took her across the road and laid her down gently on the pavement. As fresh air met her face, she began to cough and choke. She opened her eyes a slit. Lots of people were crowding round by now. One person put a cushion under her head, while another wiped her face with a wet towel. Someone else held her hand and talked to her in a low, reassuring voice.

Suddenly, Chris sat down heavily on the pavement. He was holding his arm across his chest and there was blood streaming from it all down the front of his white school shirt.

'Chris!' I cried.

'Caught it on the window frame,' he groaned. He was deathly white and his eyes were closing.

'Here, son.' An old man crouched down beside him. He put a jacket round Chris' shoulders and wrapped his arm in a towel. He pushed Chris' head down between his knees to stop him fainting and turned to me. 'See that house, lassie?' He pointed. 'Go and fetch my missus.'

I was unsure what to do. Should I do what he said, or stay with Chris, or with Tonia, or see if Joe and Mum were OK? I felt sick and wobbly, and I wasn't even the one who was hurt! But then Mum was there with her arm round me, and the man's wife came running out of the house anyway. And then, with a screech of brakes, an ambulance pulled up, and expert hands were there to look after us all.

I burst into tears, then, and finally so did Mum. But she said Tonia was alright. She'd breathed in smoke, but she wasn't burnt. Joe was the same. Mum reckoned Chris' gashed arm might need a stitch or two, and the three of them were taken off in the ambulance.

'Our job, honey,' she said, and her efficient nurse's voice had returned, 'is to tell Chris' mum that Chris and Tonia are all right, then to get the car and follow them to the hospital.'

'But what about the parking fine?' I remembered suddenly.

'Oh, I think that's a minor detail, don't you?' And she took her phone out and called Chris' family straight away.

22

When we arrived at the hospital, Mum's colleague, Eileen, was the nurse on duty. Eileen was plump and smiley with grey hair and rosy cheeks. She looked as though nothing would ever worry her, and I felt less scared straight away. We spotted Chris' family immediately – Daddo's dark head and Chris' mum's and Stuart's ginger mops.

'This your lot then, Lynn?' Eileen asked Mum.

'Well, yes. Sort of,' Mum said. 'How are they doing?'

'I don't think I'd be breaking patient confidentiality if I tell you they're all doing fine. The wee girl…'

'Tonia.'

'Aye, Tonia. She's been treated for inhaling some smoke, and a bag of toffees is helping with the shock.'

Mum smiled. 'And Joe?'

'The handsome guy? Yes, he's fine. Again, bit of smoke, but he seems remarkably cool, considering.'

Mum and I looked at each other. If only she knew.

'And Chris? He cut his arm.'

'Yes, that's a brave young man. Didn't make any fuss at all. Two stitches and a few toffees for him as well. Brother and sister, they say?' She looked puzzled, then added, 'Aye, well, families can be a right mixture these days, eh?'

Mum and I nodded and grinned.

The room where the three were waiting after treatment was already overcrowded, and everyone was talking at once. Tonia was sitting up on a couch next to Chris, offering sweets to everyone. Chris' arm was bandaged and he was wearing an oversized pullover. Joe was sitting on the only chair in the room, pale but smiling.

Daddo greeted me and Mum like long-lost friends and shook our hands vigorously.

'We want to thank you and your friend here,' Chris' mum said, indicating Joe. 'What would have happened to our wee girl without you all?' Her voice wobbled and she blinked hard.

'And Chris,' I said.

'Yes, well done, our lad,' Daddo added.

'My brother, the hero,' Stuart said with a sideways smile, and Chris gave him a friendly punch.

'Now steady on, or I'll be having my pullover back.'

But their banter was cut short by Nurse Eileen, who came in with a policewoman in uniform. 'Sorry to interrupt,' Eileen said, 'but this is Freya, and she'd like a word with each of you.'

Everyone fell silent, and Freya smiled round at all of us, especially Tonia. 'I'm sorry to put you all through this, when you'd probably rather go home and get some tea! But it's important to get the facts straight before you forget anything.'

She wanted to take each of us, one or two at a time, into an office that wasn't being used. She started with

Chris, and his mum went in with him. When they'd gone, Daddo sat on the couch and pulled Tonia onto his lap and they rocked gently together, swaying while he hummed. Stuart perched beside them, and Mum and I leaned on a wall next to Joe.

Finally, Daddo said, 'Alright, kiddo?'

Tonia nodded and unwrapped another sweet.

'So,' he went on, gently, 'what happened?' His expression was tense and anxious.

'I heard them, see,' Tonia explained. 'Outside the café, when I went with Chris, ages ago, and they knew.'

'Knew what, pet?'

'Knew I'd heard them.'

'Heard them what?'

'Heard them saying how they'd start a fire in a shop and then get reward money an' stuff.'

'Reward money?' Daddo looked appalled, but Tonia, sitting on his lap and leaning against his chest, carried on with her story.

'Yeah. For phoning the firefighters. And Nick – he's the big brother – he said they were helping the shop owners, because if their shop burnt down, they'd get money. *Inshoorance* money.' She paused. 'Daddo, what's inshoorance money?'

'An insurance company charges you a little money regularly, to kind of look after your property, then pays you a lot if you need it. Usually people don't need it, so the company keeps it, but…'

I could tell Tonia wasn't really listening. She was frowning and her lip began to tremble. 'They said they'd hurt me if I told.' Tonia sniffed. 'But then they said they'd buy me presents if I'd help them, because they're too big to climb through small windows and stuff, and I'm small and very good at gymnastics.'

'Huh. Bribery and corruption,' Stuart muttered.

'You're *excellent* at gymnastics,' Daddo said to Tonia. 'What did they give you?'

'Well, a pencil case, and a cuddly lamb, and…'

'Was this while I was at work, or since the holidays started, or…'

'They made me say I was at Miranda's, and they gave me presents to give to Miranda, too, so that she wouldn't tell on me.'

'Miranda?' Daddo said, confused.

'Daddo, Miranda lives only just up the road from us,' Stuart interrupted. 'Mum lets Tonia go on her own. No roads to cross.'

'Yeah,' Tonia went on. 'But Miranda refused to be my friend any more, and I was fed up with telling fibs. I wanted to live in the light. Like they said at Lighthouse. So I… so I…' Tonia burst into tears.

'You told them you were going to tell the police?' Stuart suggested.

Tonia shook her head. 'No. I said I'd tell my mum.'

'Same difference,' I thought. Chris always said his mum could be fiery. Stuart and Daddo smiled at each other.

Daddo waited a moment till her sobs subsided, then asked, 'But today?'

'It was that big boy.'

'Nick?'

'No, the one with the tattoo. He's even worse than Nick.'

I thought of the gang at the disco, then the boys on the beach when Joe appeared, juggling.

Tonia sat up and frowned. 'He made me get on the bus into town. He said if I yelled, he'd twist my arm. Then he said he'd buy me a big present if I did a good job.' She rubbed her arm. 'He took me into that shop and said, "See what happens to sneaks!" There was lots of cardboard boxes and he struck a match, then he shut the door on me.' Daddo shuddered and pulled her close again.

I looked at Joe. He was pale but calm and listening intently.

'Nick argued with him,' Tonia said, 'and they started to fight. I could hear them. Then Adam – he's not the worst one – he started to scream and cry and Nick told him to shut up and…'

Her lip trembled again. Daddo said, 'Shh, shh. It's alright. You're safe now, and the police won't let those boys do it any more.'

I thought of what Chris had told me about Adam, how he'd chosen to do his project on the fire in Edinburgh; how he'd read about the fire in Mr Kowalski's shop, and I wondered about Ahmed's dad's shop. It dawned on me – almost too late – that Adam had always had a fascination for fire. He had betrayed us – Chris and me, and Joe and Mum. Maybe Nick had told him to. Adam always seemed to do what his big brother told him.

Freya came back in, then, with Chris and his mum, and asked Daddo to go with Tonia. Chris was pale but smiling. 'She's very kind,' his mum told us all. 'Very gentle. Knows her stuff.'

'What I don't understand,' I began, 'was why Adam chose *today* to tell Mr Bruce about Joe. How did he even *know* about Joe?'

'I presented my project,' Chris said, 'and he must have overheard me and Ruth talking, and guessed where I'd got some of my information from.'

Joe lifted his head slowly and opened his eyes wide. 'At Lighthouse,' he said, 'Tonia say she want to live in light. She not like telling lies. She tell them *no more lies*. They want... remake? Review? Re...'

'Revenge?' I suggested.

'Yes. Revenge.'

'I tell her, me too. I not like lies. Tonia say she want to live the Jesus way. In the light.'

Mum and I felt for each other's hands and held on tight. Chris' mum was looking at Joe with a puzzled frown – she hadn't been to Lighthouse, after all – but Chris looked at me and half-smiled.

When Daddo and Tonia returned, Freya asked to speak to me and Mum. Chris' family needed to go home, so we said goodbye as we went into the office, and Joe was left alone. We told our version of the events of the day, which didn't take long.

Finally, Freya asked to speak to Joe. Mum wanted to accompany him, but Freya said politely but very firmly that she wanted to speak to Joe on his own. Mum sat down and let out an exhausted sigh. I perched on the couch.

There was a small window in the room, high up, and I could just see the sky and a branch moving in the breeze. A shaft of sunlight lit up a picture on the wall – a tranquil scene of a cornfield and a distant harvester, very different from real life. For us, at any rate.

The August sun doesn't set until late in Scotland. It must have been nearly eight o'clock.

'Mum, I'm starving,' I said suddenly. 'Can we get a takeaway on the way home?'

23

'Did you see Chris at school?' Mum asked the following afternoon.

'No, he and Tonia were off school today, but we texted. He says he'll have to miss swimming training for a couple of weeks, but he's OK.'

'And Tonia?'

'He said she's OK as well, but they won't let her go anywhere on her own now, not even round to Miranda's.'

'Yeah. I can imagine.' Mum stopped chopping vegetables and gazed out of the window. Then she said, 'I think we owe them all a bit of an explanation. Why don't we suggest meeting them for a lunch barbecue? We could go to Portobello Beach tomorrow if it's fine.'

'Yeah! Maybe we could take my stunt kite, too?'

'It's a deal! Why don't you phone Chris and ask if they're all free?'

'I will. And Joe, too?'

'Of course. Can't leave out the star player!'

The beach was always breezy, and that Saturday was no exception. Mum and I prepared salads – my speciality is always carrot and cucumber sticks – and loaded the picnic box with spicy chicken wings, sausages and burgers. Mum had bought a couple of disposable barbecues. Chris' mum had promised to buy ice creams for dessert.

We picked up Joe from the flat. He had a bag with cartons of juice and plastic cups.

Mum had taken me to Portobello Beach soon after we had arrived in Edinburgh, but in the early spring it had been huge, windswept and deserted. Now, in August, I wondered if it would be busy. 'How're we going to find them all on the beach?' I said.

'It's not really beach weather,' Mum said, looking up at the grey, overcast sky. 'It won't be crowded, but it'll be ideal for kite-flying.'

She was right. When we got there, there were people walking on the promenade, but very few were on the beach. It was easy to spot Chris' family, sheltering from the wind behind a breakwater, and Crackers running around in joyful circles.

We laid out blankets to sit on, and Daddo had put up a canvas wind-shield, held firm with big wooden tent pegs. Stuart and his mum got to work lighting the barbecues in a sheltered position, and Joe poured juice for everyone.

Chris and I ran out together to the middle of the beach, to the windiest part, with my kite.

'It's huge,' he said. 'How do you get it started?'

'Easy,' I said. 'You can help me.' I propped the kite upright and let out some of the spool. 'Hold that in position for me for a moment.' I backed up fifty metres or so and held the control with both hands. 'Are you ready? When I say go, hold it up as high as you can.'

I gave the word and he stretched up and the kite soared above us. I played out more string and it flew higher and higher. I tugged gently from side to side and let it swoop like an eagle. Chris watched it, entranced, but I looked away for a moment. I could see Joe and Daddo standing beside the barbecues, deep in conversation.

'Wow! It's beautiful,' Chris breathed. 'And easy. I had a kite ages ago – not a stunt kite, just a basic one – and I could never get it to stay up, even when I ran like mad and tugged my hardest.'

'I know. It's easy-peasy. Do you want a go?' I handed the control to him, and he quickly learned to manoeuvre the huge bird from side to side, but after a short while it hurt his injured arm, so he handed it back. Then Mum called us for food, so I wound the kite in and we joined everyone else. Mum and Chris' mum were sitting together, chatting, while Daddo stood with Joe. Stuart and Tonia handed out burgers and hot dogs. Eventually everyone sat down.

Crackers, enticed by delicious smells, pushed into the middle of the blankets, shaking wet sand over everyone. We squealed and pushed him away until eventually Stuart tied him to the breakwater, where he whined and looked pathetic for a few minutes. Finally, he lay down, sulking, with his back to us. Mum zipped up her jacket, and that made me notice how chilly it was. Summer in Scotland! I remembered how we used to complain about the unbearable heat of Egypt in August.

Daddo was sitting with one arm round Tonia, and his burger in the other hand. Once he'd finished, he shifted his position and stood up. He cleared his throat as if he was about to make a speech. I imagined him with a glass of wine, proposing a toast. There was a general shuffling and pause in the chatter. Everyone looked up.

Daddo smiled and said, 'We'd like to thank Joe again for saving our girl. But he's been explaining a few things to me, and I think he'd like to tell you himself.'

Joe stood up beside Daddo. 'Very happy to help,' he began. 'And now also, very happy because no more hiding.' Chris lifted his head up sharply and looked towards me, eyebrows raised. I shrugged in reply.

Joe continued, 'When I come here – er *came* here – I very sick. Very sad. But Lynn and Ruth,' he turned to Mum, then me, 'they very kind. Help me very much. And Chris and Ruth, they teach me English. Thank you.' He bowed. 'But I know I make big problem for them. Now I understand. I must register. I must be legal. Honest. Telling truth. Lighthouse living.'

'Yeah!' Tonia agreed, jumping up. Crackers, catching the general excitement, stood up, too, and shook himself vigorously.

'We learn,' Joe said, putting a hand on Tonia's shoulder, 'we learn to tell truth. Not to hide in shadows. Now we live in light. We want to live the Jesus way.'

'Yeah,' Tonia agreed. 'I told the Somerfields – no more fibs!'

'Yes,' Joe agreed. 'If she not tell truth, all this fires,' he waved his arm in a circle, 'all this bad things not stop.'

Yes, I realised. Tonia had threatened to tell the truth, and in doing so she had put herself in real danger. But if she hadn't, there might have been even more fires. I looked round at everyone. Mum was smiling. Chris' mum and Daddo were staring at Joe, but with the hint of a smile. Tonia was jiggling up and down and grinning. Stuart was clearly puzzled. He had a hand on Crackers, and he was looking from Joe to Tonia and back. Chris grinned at me.

Joe continued, 'Now I am strong, and I will go for interview at refugee office. Maybe I go to England, then come back to Scotland. Freya, the police officer, she not ask me anything about my papers. I was surprised. She only ask about fire. But I not afraid of police no more.'

Mum chipped in. 'My husband always said Joe would go far. And now Joe's ahead of me in going the right way about things. I wanted to see him stronger before he registered, but now I realise I went about it in the wrong way.' She looked a bit sad. 'I should have trusted the authorities – and God. But now I'm certain Joe will be fine.'

There were general murmurs of approval, and I shuffled along the blanket until I could hold Mum's hand. 'Did you know what he was going to say?' I whispered.

'No, but I suspected,' she said.

Joe must have heard. 'Is not so far,' he reassured her. 'I will come back to visit. And anyway, Oliver need flat again soon. But I never forget Lynn and Ruth. Or Chris. Or any of my friends. Thank you.' He bowed again.

'But after that, Joe,' Daddo said, '*when* you have refugee status, what do you plan to do?'

'Well, I need to learn English more gooder – er, better – and then maybe I teach maths in a college. Not university, I think. Not like Damascus. But I help young people who not do well in school. Who want to do trade – plumber, carpenter. Need maths for job.'

'Excellent,' Daddo said, laying a hand on Joe's shoulder. 'We should drink to that! But in the absence of a glass of champagne…'

'I'll go and buy us some ice creams!' Chris' mum filled in. 'Chris, come and help me to carry them.' And they went off across the beach to the kiosk on the promenade.

When they came back, Chris settled down on the blanket beside me and we ate our cones in silence for a moment or two. Then I asked him, 'What do you think?'

'What about?'

'Anything. What Joe said. What Daddo said. What Tonia told the boys.'

'Joe is a very brave man, so I think he'll be OK, even if getting refugee status isn't straightforward.'

'Even if he has to go to one of those places where Mum says the neighbours aren't friendly?'

'Yeah. Even then. He'll make friends there, as well.'

'And how did Adam know about Joe? And why do you think he told Mr Bruce?'

'Adam must have overheard us. He realised you and I were keeping Joe a secret, and he knew Tonia is my sister. When she told them she wouldn't help them any more, Adam knew how to get his own back. He just wanted me to get told off.'

'But that horrible boy – Nick's mate. Why did he shut Tonia in the shop?'

Chris shuddered. 'I reckon he's in a whole different league. What started as a stupid trick turned thoroughly evil. That boy's older than Nick, and much older than Adam. I think he was the ringleader. Tonia said he and Nick were arguing. Remember how upset Adam was? I think it all just got out of hand.'

I had a sudden thought. 'What d'you think Mr Bruce will say?'

'Ha! I'll have to speak to him on Monday when I go back to school. But if my little sister is determined to tell the truth, I don't have much choice, do I?' He grinned.

While Joe's juggling
I've been struggling
To read Luke's book.
Just look
Says Ruth.
Find real truth.
He'll show you how
To live life now
The Jesus way.

Notes

Chapter 2
The Bible verse mentioned here is part of Psalm 18:2: 'My God is my protection, and with him I am safe' (Good News Translation).

Chapter 14
Ruth's mum told her: 'Don't let the sun go down while you are still angry' (Ephesians 4:26, New Living Translation).

Chapter 16
You can find the story of Nicodemus visiting Jesus at night in John chapter 3.

Chapter 17
At rugby matches, Scotland supporters like to sing the song 'O Flower of Scotland'. The song actually celebrates Scotland's victory in a battle in 1314. Then, the Scottish army was fighting against England but now it's just used to encourage the Scottish team.

Chapter 19

The verse that Daniel remembers is John 14:6: 'I am the way, the truth, and the life' (Good News Translation). Nathan encourages Chris with the verse from Luke 11:9: 'seek, and you will find' which goes on: 'knock, and the door will be opened to you' (Good News Translation).

All through the book, we learn about the magnificent city of Edinburgh, in Scotland. What great things have you learned about it, in this story? If you're interested, check out these websites:

https://scotlandwelcomesyou.com/greyfriars-bobby/
https://edinburgh.org
https://www.theforthbridges.org

Think!

Have you enjoyed this book? Has it challenged you about certain things? Perhaps it has encouraged you to…

- Think more about the plight of refugees
- Realise how important it is to say sorry to friends
- See how 'living in the light' is really important
- Anything else?

What does 'living in the light' really mean? Perhaps, like Chris, you are still working out what it means to live the Jesus way. If you like, you can ask the author, Helen, by writing to the publisher, Instant Apostle. Drop an email to info@instantapostle.com.